AFTERSHOCKS

AFTER SHOCKS

An
Anthology of
So-Cal Horror

**Edited by
Jeremy Lassen**

fREAk pRESs
San Diego || San Francisco

Introduction © 2000 by Jeremy Lassen
"Bodywork" © 2000 by Christa Faust
"Mourning Glory" © 2000 Michael Scott Bricker
"Street Runes" © 2000 by Stephen Woodworth
"A Flock of Drunk Witches" © 2000 by Dana Vander Els
"El Cazador" © 2000 by Lisa Morton
"Born to Wear Black" © 2000 by Denise Dumars
"The Infant Kiss" copyright 2000 by Robert Guffey
"Driving the Last Spike" © 2000 by Brian Hodge
"The Heart in Darkness" © 2000 by Nancy Holder
"Frayed Seams" © 2000 by Michael D. Frounfelter
"Parallel Highways" © 2000 by James Van Pelt
"Lies for Dessert" © 2000 by Jak Koke

First·Printing
ISBN 0-9700097-0-4

fREAk pRESs
www.freakpress.com

After Shocks is dedicated to **Liza Marie S. Erpelo**, without whose work and encouragement **fREAk pRESs** would not exist.

Special thanks go to **David Berl-Hahn**, everyone at **Mysterious Galaxy** in San Diego, **Borderlands Books** in San Francisco, and **Know Knew Books** in Palo Alto.

Finally, thanks to all the contributors to *After Shocks* for their visions of Southern California...

Contents

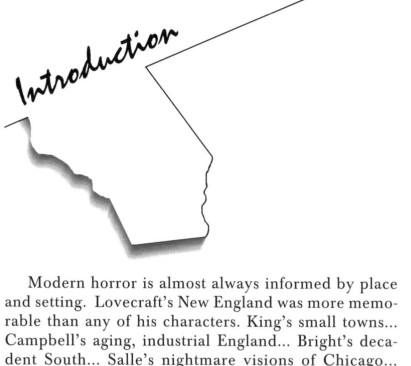

Modern horror is almost always informed by place and setting. Lovecraft's New England was more memorable than any of his characters. King's small towns... Campbell's aging, industrial England... Bright's decadent South... Salle's nightmare visions of Chicago... Lansdale's twisted Texas... The list is endless. As disparate as the above writers are, they all manage to create a recognizable place and time. Places that their real-life denizens recognize – places that are both comfortingly familiar and terrifyingly unique. King's New England will never be mistaken for Lovecraft's New England. This is the magic of modern horror. It creates worlds that we recognize. At the same time these worlds are horribly and terrifyingly different from the one we choose to interact with on a daily basis. Horrible because they speak truths we rarely acknowledge. Terrifying because just maybe they are more real than the artificially constructed realities we choose to live in each day.

It is problematic to base an anthology around a particular region. The stories may run together, simply repeating the same tired clichés. Or they may be so wildly divergent that no sense of place and time is created, instead reflecting the same hollow sets of a million generic TV sitcoms. Ahh... TV. A shared hallucination depicting humanity's peculiar hopes, dreams and depravities. This points to the crux of the problem with a Southern California anthology. So-Cal is instantly identified with Hollywood. There is no getting around the L.A. mythology. During the course of assembling this book, I received numerous references to the "Hollywood" anthology I was putting together, even though I had clearly stated *After Shocks* was not about Hollywood, but rather about So-Cal as a region. The old telephone game always pares things down to essentials.

Nonetheless, So-Cal will always be much more than Hollywood. The mix of cultures and ethnicities is overwhelming. The Pacific Rim, Central and South America and every state in the union have contributed to So-Cal's cultural makeup. Diversity may be a buzzword in political and academic circles, but it's a reality in So-Cal. This diversity extends to the realm of socioeconomics as well, with vast entrenched classes living side by side, yet having completely different expectations and values. The homeless, the migrant workers and the working poor in their barrios, ghettos and shantytowns, the middle classes in their suburban fortresses, and the obscenely wealthy in their estates and mansions: All of these make up parts of the So-Cal mosaic. The physical and psychological space between these classes is filled with razor wire, the corpses of those who have *tried* to cross over and the memories of those who *have* crossed in *both* directions.

Does a region of immigrants and transplants have a distinct set of dreams and desires? Can So-Cal's notions of place and identity expand beyond the clichés and create a reality that is at once recognizable and unique? When I began this project, I believed the answer was "yes." The stories I received confirmed this belief. The writers who have contributed to this volume have moved me and impressed me with their visions of So-Cal. I hope they do the same for you.

Jeremy Lassen
San Diego, CA

Bodywork

Christa Faust

Anna hadn't even wanted to go to the car show. She told herself that when Ruby called she would bow out, make some excuse. But when the phone shattered the hot stillness of her un-air-conditioned studio, pulling her up from thin, twisted sleep, she knew before she laid a hand on the receiver that she would give in, just like she always did.

"Morning, sleepy," Ruby's voice, movie star husky and inescapable in the vulnerable curves of Anna's ear. "You ready yet?"

"Ruby, I..."

"I'll be there in 15."

She arrived in 10, barely giving Anna time to mix instant coffee with hot water from the tap and rinse the night's suffocating sweat from her skin.

"It's a fucking oven in here!" Ruby announced, flinging her plastic purse on Anna's rumpled fold-out bed and immediately ripping down the blanket that had been hung over the single window to block out the smog-magnified L.A. sun. Like the sun, Ruby was an unstoppable force, goddess-like in her retrotrash finery and stiletto heels and Anna knew better than to get in her way. She was Anna's only friend.

"This apartment sucks," she said, dabbing sweat from her perfectly painted face with a lace hankie baring someone else's initials. "It's like a bad hotel room."

She was right, of course, but Anna didn't care. No matter where she lived, her surroundings had always been spartan, incidental. A way station without identity. The Salvation Army furniture was here when she came and would stay when she left. The fold-out bed, the tacky coffee table, the yellowed lamps. Nothing matched and yet everything had the same sad flavor, like a cluster of drunks in a shitty hotel bar. The carpet was thick and awful, the color of a spoiled orange. Against this tawdry backdrop, Anna stood naked except for a thin, flowered towel bought in a pack of three at Pic 'N Save, feeling Ruby's thickly lined eyes sizing her up as they always did and feeling inadequate as she always did.

"Let me do your makeup, honey." This in a softer voice, conciliatory.

Anna nodded, content as always to allow Ruby's ritual revision. Ruby regularly cut and colored her hair as well, but no matter how new and fabulous she was when the magic of irons and blow-dryers was complete, a week later, Anna always looked like her plain old self again.

Digging through her purse, Ruby extracted the ritual tools, mascara wand and eyebrow pencil and slut-red lipstick. Holding Anna's face between thumb and forefinger, she went to work reshaping her thin lips into a sexy pout, darkening her ashy pale lashes and redefining her grey eyes with some mysterious black liquid that gave them a feline, bad-girl shape. Not satisfied with the stringy tumble of Anna's recently bleached hair, she herded it up into an impromptu semibeehive secured with pins and lacquer and the force of Ruby's will. When she was done, Anna felt new. Sexy even. She didn't object to the suggestion that she wear that silly leopard-print dress Ruby had bought for her during one of many manic thrift store binges. Stockings and boots and the transformation was complete. Studying her reflection, studying who she had become, she smiled a little. The girl in the mirror would have fun at a car show.

"C'mon, already," Ruby said, impatient nails digging into Anna's bare upper arm. "You look fine. I wouldn't let you look bad."

So here she was, sweat trickling down the channel of her spine on this poison-hot September afternoon that smelled of exhaust and carne asada and cheap cologne. They were somewhere like Pomona or El Monte, So-Cal anyburb. Surrounded by uninspired fast food sprawl and dying palm trees, the show was like a bubble of otherworldly fantasy, defiant in the midst of grinding mundanity.

The cars lined up like playmates, hoods up, doors open, pornographically spread above strategic mirrors that revealed every proud modification, every hidden mechanism. Gaudy, fantastical, and vaguely menacing, they didn't even seem to come from the same planet as the humble hatchbacks that clogged the rush-hour freeways. Their immaculate chromed engines flashed seductively. Deep-glossed paint jobs in unearthly colors like Microflake Tangerine or Black Plum Pearl, glistening like half-sucked candy in the vicious sun. Complex hydraulics tilted their rococo chassis in a bizarre, mechanical come-on. Hoods were painted with Aztec gods and girls in bikinis, demons and eagles and tumbling dice. Many were surrounded by trophies and arching golden letters that read things like *BOMB SQUAD* and *LOW 'N SLOW*. And the men who made them what they are stood close, pride filling their chests as they made small, tender adjustments, wiping away the evidence of their touch with soft cloth. The analogy of a lover's touch came to Anna's mind and was immediately discarded. The relationship between machine and maker was a thousand times more profound. Anna wondered what it would be like to be touched like that.

Beyond an open area set up with hash-marked poles designed to measure the height that each vehicle's front end could be lifted off the ground, there stood a second double row of bizarre creations that seemed even farther removed from the constraints of function. And at the end of the long row was a machine that drew Anna to it, seducing her with its outrageous impracticality, its extreme, kaleidoscopic beauty. The proudly displayed interior was a plush riot of purple and green velvet, complete with TV, VCR, stereo and full bar. Like a porno-movie set, yet somehow pristine, as if the vulgarity of human flesh had never touched it. The engine was a work of art, every humble component replaced by glittering gold and virgin chrome. Surrounded by a forest of trophies, this machine was queen of the show and seemed to know it.

Taking a step closer, Anna felt her breath catch in her belly. She no longer felt the heat, the blistering sun. She lost herself in the gorgeous convolutions of mechanical poetry, in the ghostly patterns that skimmed the glossy surfaces of a cool, beetle-green paint job that looked deep enough to drown in. A low, bassline pulse began to beat inexplicably between her legs.

Then Ruby, shattering the moment with her bright, intrusive personality.

"Time to hustle, honey." Arm snaking around Anna's waist to pull her reluctantly away. She had no idea how long she had been standing there.

On the way to her car, Ruby decided to brave the row of stinking Porta Potties, leaving Anna standing alone and vaguely horny beside a '59 Impala whose candy-apple skin made her want to taste it. She felt weirdly unfocused, spacey and filled to overflowing with curious inorganic desire. Waiting dumbly, she became aware of someone standing close to her. A sawed-off Latina, slightly shorter than Anna, compact and muscular with dark skin and blue-black hair cut butch-short in a slick, old-fashioned style. She wore high waisted pants held up by suspenders and a man's undershirt, big espresso nipples clearly visible through the thin white fabric. There were delicate lacy designs like silver tattoos winding around her sleek forearms, almost as if some kind of metal wire had been embedded in the skin. Black wraparound sunglasses hid her eyes. Her dress shoes were perfect, seeming to intimidate the dust with their pristine gloss.

"I saw you looking at the cars," she said. Her sugar-syrup voice held only a teasing trace of Mexican accent.

"They're all so beautiful," Anna said, just to say something. She was sweating, dizzy from the sun and from the wicked darts of light thrown off the coils of exposed engines. She was suddenly sure that this woman could tell how turned on she was, that she could smell it somehow.

"You could be too," the woman said.

For a second Anna thought she had misheard. Her heart skidded but she forced herself to remain passive under this sudden scrutiny. The woman reached out and took Anna's hand but instead of bringing it to her lips as it seemed for a moment that she might, she turned it palm up and began systematically working the joints in Anna's fingers as if testing their limits. Though she couldn't see her eyes, Anna could feel the woman sizing her up, taking in every part of her with the detached speculation of a careful consumer. She found that she wanted anything this woman wanted to do to her.

The woman pressed a business card into Anna's hand. Flustered, Anna licked her lips and clenched her fist around the little rectangle of cheap paper. She was suddenly afraid that Ruby would see it and try to take it away.

"Are you a mechanic?" she asked, realizing that she did not want the woman to go away, that she didn't want Ruby to come back.

The woman flexed the corner of her mouth as if privately amused.

"Yeah," she said. "You could say that."

Then, as if Anna's guilt had evoked her like a vengeful genie, Ruby appeared, freshly lipsticked and frowning.

"EX-cuse me," she interjected, eyes reduced to jealous slits. "We're leaving." Heavy emphasis on *we.*

The mechanic gave Anna a last hard stare and then shrugged and walked away.

"What was that about?" Ruby asked, possessive now.

"Nothing," Anna lied. "She was just trying to sell me something."

It was the first time she had ever lied to Ruby.

It wasn't until the mechanic was long gone and Ruby was distracted with car keys that Anna was able to focus her eyes enough to read. The crumpled card had only one word printed in simple capital letters above the smaller phone number.

It said: *BODYWORK.*

With a not-unpleasant shiver, Anna slipped it into her wallet.

Slumped in the passenger seat of Ruby's big black Riviera, Anna pretended to listen to her friend's gossipy monologue. Ruby was in "The Industry," a make-up artist who made a living covering up celebrity imperfections. Anna, on the other hand, was no one. So she nodded gravely at the appropriate places in the litany of sacred names, this latest tapestry of scars from breast implants or needles or suicide attempts. Bruises inflicted by thug boyfriends or the ravages of starvation in a land of plenty. Ruby was speeding, as she always did, cranking the massive steel boat up to 95 as they blew past rabbity commuters and execs with cell phones and housewives trying to convince themselves that they were bold adventurers cruising the Serengheti in their Suburban Utility Vehicles rather than baby slaves on the way home from day-care in glorified station wagons. Normally, Anna would be terrified, heart between her teeth while Ruby drove with one hand, casually cutting people off and flipping them the bird. Ruby had obviously already forgotten the mechanic, but Anna hadn't. She couldn't. She was barely aware of anything outside of the faint residual tingle in her fingers, the slow burn of that simple business card hidden inside her wallet.

Getting back to her building had become a major pain in the ass ever since the cops had blocked off her street at each intersection with steel poles driven into the asphalt, chopping it into inaccessible segments. This was supposed to prevent cruising and drug trafficking, but for Anna, it only prevented Ruby from dropping her off in front of her place. Ruby said she had to rush off to some kind of shoot, so Anna walked that extra half a block alone, very aware of her leopard dress and fishnet stockings and slightly disappointed that Ruby had not wanted to come up. She never seemed to want to come up anymore.

Surprisingly, no one hassled Anna as she walked and she found herself impulsively continuing past the sad aqua lunch box of her building and following Yucca down towards Vine. A tight cluster of grim and unshaven men in front of the Pla-Boy liquor store swiveled dead eyes to follow her, offering up a few half-assed whistles, but she barely heard them, wrapped up as she was in the workings of her muscles and bones, the mechanisms of her body. Visions of hot chrome and the mechanic's touch and she kept putting one foot in front of the other, instinctively avoiding the dying fever of the Boulevard and looping around on Fountain. The idea of being cooped up in that tiny room seemed unendurable and it was still far too early to sleep, with the sun only just committing its bloody suicide dive into the Pacific Ocean. So she kept on moving, kept on walking.

To be a pedestrian in Los Angeles is to be subhuman, beneath notice. Something to be glanced briefly through tinted windows and then forgotten. Only homeless people walked, pushing shopping carts filled with tin cans and old Christmas decorations and Academy Awards. Homeless and the invisible alien workforce that kept the city's gardens lush and the toilets clean and the children diapered, greasing the wheels of luxury with their exotic blood. Homeless, aliens, and Anna.

Her funky hairdo was melting in the heat, coming undone now that she was out of range of Ruby's touch-ups, so she surrendered to entropy, pulling the pins out and tossing them into the street unmindful of the sticky snarls they left behind. Her red lipstick was mostly faded and she wiped the rest away on the back of her hand. She felt as if as she was becoming less defined, more ephemeral with every step, as if Ruby's modifications were all that had held her anchored in the real world. She felt like a ghost amid the mingled fragrances of sickly night-blooming flowers cultivated in fenced-off yards and split-open trash bags fought over by stray dogs. Of spicy cooking and the hopeless, rusty metal smell of bad neighborhoods in the summer.

Without thinking, she hooked up Las Palmas and found herself drawn in to the pale glow that surrounded the narrow newsstand. Just above the fleshy jumble of porn publications was a modest selection of Hot Rod and Lowrider magazines. She could not resist picking one up and thumbing through its bright pages. Captivated by the lush colors and flagrant frivolity displayed within, Anna again lost track of time until the surly cashier informed her of the five-minute browsing limit. She was just about to set the magazine back in its place when her eye snagged on a page of what appeared to be personal messages. There among declarations of love, pleas for second chances, or requests for prison pen pals was that word again, in quiet letters that hit Anna like a stealthy rabbit punch.

BODYWORK

And beneath that:

"*The next step.*"

Then the number.

With shaking hands, Anna bought the magazine with the last of that month's spare change. She felt furtive and nervous, as if she were buying *Shaved Nymphos* or *Barely Legal.* She had to breathe deep, force herself to walk slowly away.

As she made her way back home, clutching her purchase to her chest, her heart began to slow and her mind drifted. She was content to let it go, to kill time with fantasies of engines and of being loved.

The next day Anna had to work. She worked in a copy shop, making endless Xeroxes of desperate spec scripts to be thrust into the faces of annoyed Hollywood royalty in the men's rooms of trendy restaurants. These writers usually had three names and were always painfully optimistic like beaten dogs that still keep slinking back for more abuse. Sometimes they would practice their "pitches" on Anna while the machines obediently spat out three-holed pages. She would put on her retail robot face and nod politely and try to say something like, "I'm sure Mr. Schwartzenegger will love it."

But that day, her mind was elsewhere. The latest three-named writer had given up trying to talk to her and was instead chatting up one of the barbies who had come in to pick up zed cards. Anna could barely force herself to complete the brainless tasks her meager job demanded. All she could think of was the joints in her fingers and the magazine and the terrible emotion that curled around her heart, fluctuating between desire and panic. Ruby called and tried to get her to come out after work, but Anna said she was tired. She was amazed at her sudden resistant strength and even more amazed when Ruby let it go. She had to hold on tightly to the edge of the counter, unsteady and afraid the world had been secretly rearranged.

Zeke, her cartoon-exuberant co-worker, had been teasing her mercilessly all day as she screwed up one order after another.

"So what's his name?" Zeke would ask repeatedly, clacking his tongue-piercing against his teeth in a way that he knew annoyed her.

When she refused to answer, he would sulk, hiding behind an *Urban Primitives* magazine whenever there was a rush of customers and leaving her to fend for herself up front. When he could no longer avoid help-ing people, he would leave the magazine open to some close-up photo of spiky genitalia.

In the lull just after lunch, she was counting out change for a woman who came in every day with pho-tos of famous actors that she would photocopy, gluing her own cut-out head onto the bodies of the actors' girlfriends. When she laid the last coin in the woman's sweaty glitter-nailed hand, Anna noticed Zeke's magazine had tumbled off the counter. Squatting to pick it up and maybe even toss it in the trash, she saw that word again, unmistakable. *BODYWORK*. Same phrase, same number, but this time lurking amidst advertisements for needles and niobium. Anna dropped the magazine as if it were on fire.

It took her almost a week to break down and call.

"Yeah," a voice said on the other end, picking up after a single ring. She had no idea if it was the same person. Her heart was beating far too fast. Zeke was staring at her with his tongue out and so she turned away and pulled the phone cord out as long as it could stretch. She felt vaguely faint and had to force herself to speak.

"My name is Anna," she said, appalled at the tentative squeak that had replaced her voice. "We met last week at the car show..."

She trailed off, hanging terrified over the abyss of silence between them. She thought she could hear the sound of hydraulics in the background and the cicada whir of electric lug wrenches. Just when she was sure she could not stand another second, the voice spoke and she couldn't believe she didn't recognize her the first time.

"Give me your address."

In a teenage-girl gush, she told the mechanic to pick her up here at the shop when she got off her shift. When she finished reciting the address, the mechanic hung up without saying goodbye.

She set the phone back in its cradle and took a deep

breath. A customer was saying something to her, but she couldn't hear him. She left him standing stupid at the counter with a handful of grubby singles and ran to the toilet.

Squatting with her back against the door and her pants around her knees, she masturbated viciously, the cheap weave of her Kwik Kopy T-shirt clenched between her teeth. She found a curious fantasy flooding into her consciousness, a dream of silver skin and well-oiled joints, of a perfect, impossible body. In her mind, the beauty of the car show became her own, the organic curves surrendering to the superior strength of chrome and fiberglass. She came suddenly, banging her head against the door hard enough to send a shower of sparks across her vision like the starry splash created when a welder's torch meets metal.

The mechanic was exactly on time, pulling into the lot in a revamped midnight-blue Studebaker that turned heads for blocks. She got out and came around to open the passenger-side door for Anna. Her sharply cut pachuco drape was smooth, supernaturally unrumpled in spite of the oppressive heat. Anna felt wretched and unlovely in her work clothes with her hair pulled back in a sloppy knot. Unable to speak, she bowed her head and slipped into the car. The cavernous interior smelled of pomade and leather and hot steel. The sound of the heavy door slamming was as final as a guillotine blade.

Studying the mechanic surreptitiously as she drove, Anna thought that she was in love with her, that she must be. That this desire, this panicked hunger that seemed to own every part of her, must be what people meant when they talked about "crimes of passion."

She wanted to press kisses to the flawless gloss of the mechanic's two-toned shoes as they spoke to the Studebaker's pedals, coaxing obedience from the beautiful, high-strung machine. The mechanic never said a word, seeming to be an extension of the car, a modern-day centaur. Anna found that she felt an equal desire to touch both the car, the curved faces of the gages, the cool texture of the tiny chain-link steering wheel and the mechanic, the strong angle of her jaw and her thick, callused fingers. She still wore the impenetrable black shades, cutting Anna off completely from any sense of human intimacy. She didn't miss it at all. Humans lie. Machines do not.

They arrived somewhere and Anna realized abruptly that she had no idea where she was. She had told no one where she was going, and although everyone in the mini-mall parking lot in front of the copy shop had stopped to gawk at her ostentatious ride, she doubted anyone would remember the face of the driver. Instead of feeling scared, she felt comforted by this knowledge. As if fate had given her permission to disappear.

Having pulled into the scrap-littered lot of a large and seemingly abandoned garage, the mechanic came around again to open Anna's door. She felt unsteady and the mechanic seemed to know it instantly, wrapping a firm arm around Anna's waist to support her as she stood. This simple contact was incendiary. The smell of the mechanic's skin made Anna's head swim, musky sweat and burning metal, blood and copper and industrial lubricants. She leaned into her like a tired child, letting the mechanic lead her up to a small door cut high into the larger roll-up.

Inside it was surprisingly cool. The space was huge,

cathedral-like. There were cars, some covered with tarps, other exposed and vivisected like some complex experiment. Parts too, arcane and gorgeous and Anna wanted to touch everything but didn't. Instead she waited, silent, wondering.

The mechanic removed her glasses in the dimness, revealing lashless eyes like mirrors, the whole of the ball a shiny, reflective surface in which Anna could see tiny replicas of her own plain face. This barely had time to register before the mechanic took her hand again and spoke.

"I've been thinking about you," she said. "Your bones. You are perfect." She leaned closer, voice dropped low to a near whisper. "Cherry."

Anna's heart kicked into high gear, chill sweat sheening her skin.

"I...," she stammered. "I want..."

"I know," the mechanic said, scarred fingers brushing her cheekbone. "I know what you want."

She led Anna down a steep flight of cement steps, into a cramped basement workshop that was one of many, set like honeycomb cells in a vast and busy hive.

"Wait here," she instructed, leaving Anna alone and without choices.

The circular space was lit like an operating theater. In the center of the room was a strange spidery thing that resembled the love child of a medical examination table and a hydraulic lift. Tools were laid out, easily accessible. Their shapes seemed infinite, ranging from delicate scalpels and hemostats to bulky rivet guns and power drills and things that Anna had never seen. Things that hinted at unthinkable purpose. The floor was tiled, with a large drain in the center.

When the mechanic reappeared, she was dressed a loose-fitting coverall and a thick rubber apron, her strong hands sheathed in latex.

"Are you ready?" she asked, her voice almost tender.

Anna bit deeply into her lower lip. She was.

The mechanic helped her up into the cradle and webbed her in with heavy-duty cable that divided her body up into a butcher's chart of work areas. As the mechanic moved to insert a massive rubber bit into her mouth, she flinched, fearful and suddenly unsure.

"What's that?" she asked.

"It's to keep you from screaming," the mechanic told her, soothing her like a vet with a skittish horse.

"But I won't scream," she said.

The mechanic blinked her chromed eyes. Her voice was gentle but firm, like a doctor, like a parent correcting a wayward child.

"Of course you will," she said.

A long tense moment unwound between them. Anna could hear the faraway music of laboring machines, keeping time with her nervous heart. She nodded with her eyes closed and obediently opened her mouth.

A warehouse, deep in the forgotten maze of some old, industrial neighborhood. The location was secret, of course, but those who knew found it without hesitation. While the car show had been bright and open and full of sun and children, this event was private, hidden, lit with mercury lights and protected by stone-faced gang members with Chinese AK knockoffs.

Inside were the machines, each more fabulous than the last. But there was one that took the spectators' breath away with its delicate, clockwork perfection, its inventive audacity. Razor-thin frills like an air conditioner, like a wedding dress. Clear lucite covered the curved abdomen. Jealous rivals and beaming club members pressed close to view the gold-mesh and colorful rubber organs contained within. The heart-pump was raised up out of the chest cavity and housed in a complex wire cage glittering with LED displays. A transparent speculum had been inserted to give a better view of a filigreed cervix that blossomed outward like a hybrid lily. The cocked-back legs were powerful and insectoid, triple-jointed and reinforced with pistons. The back of the steel skull was porcupine-spiky with glowing fiber optics. Its name – ANATOMICA – was etched into the smoky glass eyeplate, the club name – BODYWORK – beneath in fine gold script. No one was surprised when she took first place.

"Absolutely stunning," the judge told the mechanic as he handed over an enormous trophy in a storm of camera-flash. "This is your best and most original work to date."

The other club members rushed the stage to gleefully embrace her and then stand proud for a group photo with the winning entry.

"We won, baby," the mechanic whispered, caressing her masterpiece's sleek new skull, and although Anna could no longer hear, she knew it and was happy.

Mourning Glory
Michael Scott Bricker

The dead are never conceited. They are not social climbers. They keep their opinions to themselves. They are quiet, withdrawn, and, given time, they let their appearances go. They have no affectations, no egos, and in The City of Angels, just this morning, one hundred suicides were borne into this perfection. The Mourner admired them for their Tragic Deaths, and she had watched as they dropped from apartment building balconies like bundles of laundry, had listened to the thuds as they hit the concrete below. The Church always kept suicides in mind when they designed those buildings (large, sliding windows, easy roof access, adequate dive potential), though they did not do a good job, and did not deserve recognition. Praise was reserved for the dead, and artists who had been neglected in life were to be praised most of all.

Like all Adequate Citizens, The Mourner shunned the ego, and closely adhered to the teachings of The

Church. She dared to hope that she was bad at her job too, that she was a selfish, awful person, but she harbored secret desires as well, and imagined that her neglected talents might be discovered and celebrated after her own Tragic Death. She knew that this was one of The Ten Major Character Flaws, but she strove to carry her secret to the grave, rather than to suffer the consequences of an Anonymous Death. The Mourner had booked Tasteless Entertainers for State Funerals since she had been a teen (Unsafe and Insane Fireworkers, Fightrope Walkers, Explosive Elephants), and she wanted nothing less than Grotesque Displays of Affection at her own funeral.

It had been nearly a week since The Mourner had arranged the death of a Truly Bad Artist, and like all Truly Bad Artists, this one lived in poverty, deep within The Bad Side of Town. The tracks of the People Remover ended at Miles From Nowhere, and as she stepped from the train, she saw the lines of Crack Busses. Judging from the neighborhood, she knew that this Bad Artist would be worse than most. Freaks and Low-Lives gathered around the busses, made Clandestine Drug Deals with Stolen Money, but their lack of skill and grace was as obvious as the flawed Educational System that had nurtured them. Like all Failed Junkies, they had been hand-picked, admired for their cherubic pallor and their frailty and their own addicted parents (though grudgingly so) and at an age when The Less Fortunate might have been learning to read and write, they were sent to The School of the Streets. There they had learned the Art of the Deal, but had they been more receptive, and had the Educational System been better, they might have avoided the clubs of

Corrupt Cops, and been better versed in The Art of Bribery.

To the minor credit of the Junkers (the new Aryan Oil Burner 5000, when not in the shop, was slightly more offensive than most) the air was thick with smog, so the Mourner took a deep breath, and was sad to be alive. The Sewage Carriers had just unloaded, and a poor grade of The Stuff pooled around clogged drains. It reminded The Mourner of her childhood, and although she had been raised in one of the Haughty Areas, and had been weaned on the pomp and merry-making at State Funerals, she had visited the Bad Side of Town on many occasions, and had, in fact, approved her first suicide here at the age of twelve. He had been a Failed Musician, barely thirty years old, and although Choking on Your Own Vomit had fallen out of fashion with the Artist-Drug Users, she had arranged quite a show, and the Musician had died before twelve thousand Screaming Madmen at Pabulumpalooza XXXII.

She dressed like a proper Mourner, and although her Black Duds had been made by The Worst in the Business, she was not a very good bulimic (her Hair Shirt added pounds as well) and her clothing would have been better suited to Twiggies or The Wasted. Her skin carried an unprofessional flush now and then, but she covered it with face paint, dyed and dried her hair, and dabbed a little embalming fluid behind her ears. She was not adequate at her job, but she looked functional enough, and her Little Bleak Bag added Ominous Overtones. The thick smell of sewage made her hunger for Victuals, and she noticed a Bitter Street Vendor selling Dolphin Smacks by a group of Street Bums and Filthy Little Urchins. The Bums were too deeply involved in their own hallucinations to notice her approach (they, too, had been serviced by the Crack Busses) and the Urchins ran and screamed and did somewhat creative things with shards of broken bottles. After engaging in ten minutes of Unnecessary Haggling with Language Barrier, The Mourner parted with The Immoral Buck, and the Bitter Street Vendor supplied her with a pack of Dolphin Smacks. They were fresher than they should have been, and after she had absorbed two of them through the skin of her throat, The Mourner produced her Cheap Recorder, and made the following entry:

"July twenty-first, 2107. Bitter Street Vendor, The Bad Side of Town, corner of Sloth and Gluttony. Vendor unusually chipper. Product superior. Takes pride in work. Inform Corrupt Cops. Suggest Racially-Motivated-Hate-Crime, caught on Home-Cam."

The Mourner gave herself thirty minutes in which to Fear For Her Life, witnessing Drive-Byes, making wrong turns down Dark Alleys, avoiding The Stuff with every step, and then she arrived at The Sleaze, one of the poorer no-stars hotels west of New Styx. The Neo-Fascist architecture did little to darken the mood of the old place, and despite the fact that The Sleaze was a Certified Death Trap, and that the Green Team had recently hosed the ledges and fire escapes with Disgusting Guano, the building did not look as bad as some she had seen down in The Hood. While it certainly should have been worse than it was, The Mourner had to admit that the abundance of Clip Joints and Venereal Distilleries in the area sucked character from The Sleaze, and she did not know of a cheaper place where a Family Man could get a Quadruple "X" Mind Wipe.

The Media Circus had already arrived, and they surrounded the Mourner, grinding along with their heavy Maxi-Cams on power rollers, tagging her body with tracking tabs, and if it weren't for the scheduled Random Act of Violence in the street, she might not have made her way into The Sleaze at all. An Obnoxious Tour Bus broke down in front of The Swedish Massage Paroler, and six Little Old Ladies emerged, wandered aimlessly, then were pummeled by a group of Neglected Latch Key Kids. The Media Circus responded immediately. The News Angerman joined the festivities, and used his Microphobe as a club. It was effective enough, and before long, he had stolen enough Old Lady Jewelry to buy his way out of The Big House.

The lobby of The Sleaze was as disappointing as the exterior had been, and although a Shifty Clerk hid behind the negligible safety of a barbed wire screen, and the "Hourly Rates" signs were scarred with the fruits of malicious Gunplay, The Mourner, once again, was not impressed. The Shifty Clerk ignored her as any Shifty Clerk would, and upon finding that The Descender was broken, she began to climb Another Rickety Staircase. She felt rotten wood bowing with every step, could hear The Big Fat Rats in the walls, and she stopped climbing upon reaching the third floor, where The Truly Bad Artist lived in Relative Squalor, or room thirty-two. Some Bored Rich Kids had tagged the hallway, and due to the notably offensive nature of the graffiti, The Mourner felt that The Defamation League was adequately regulating The Lower Arts.

While she had expected to find the Truly Bad Artist in a Typical Drunken Stupor, such was not the case. His door was open, the lock still broken due to the efforts of an Amateur Crook, and as she entered, he set down his brush and said, "You've come to kill me."

The Mourner sat on a crate and opened her Little Bleak Bag. "We're not uncivilized." She looked at The Sad Clown he had been painting, secretly admired its lack of depth, its faulty composition, and asked him whether or not he cared to feature Deranged Dancing Bears at his State Funeral.

"Do you enjoy your job?" The Truly Bad Artist had spent his Formative Years at Pretentious Coffee Houses, and there he had learned to Psychoanalyze From the Get-Go. Although age had softened his manner, and his goatee had grayed, he still was One Annoying Little Bastard.

The Mourner handed him a few brochures. "I think that you might find the one about Crematory Clowns apropos."

The Truly Bad Artist lived in a One-Room Pigsty, and it represented one of the worst designs to emerge from the Second Bowel Movement. The Inexplicable Rat Droppings, as well as the Ominous Plumbing, were the work of a Dishonest Architect who was thought to be a No-Talent Crook until his Tragic Death revealed Neglected Talents. "Would *you* want Crematory Clowns at *your* funeral?"

"I don't deserve Crematory Clowns. Although your paintings appear to be lousy to my untrained eye, you will certainly be discovered by Arty Blowhards after your Tragic Death. It's probable that you will become one of the Great Immortal Artists, and without my help, this will not come to pass."

"That sounded *egotistical*, don't you think?"

"I have no Ego. Ego is the Root of All Evil. It's like the Big Book says '...and then God got fed up, and abandoned humanity..."'"

"I've never cared for The One True Religion." The Artist paused, then asked, "How do you like my paintings?"

"The Sad Clown has been entered into the Registry of Bad Taste, and is now a Registered Trademark, as is The Velvet Elvis and Dogs Playing Poker. You are performing as expected."

"I spent twelve years studying Dogs Playing Poker, but I expanded upon that art form: cats, pigs, wolverines. Have you ever seen Frilled Lizards Playing Pinochle? That was mine."

"That's inconsequential."

"Permit me to show you something." The Artist dropped the brochures, stood, moved towards his Stained Mattress, and from underneath, he removed a small painting. "I wanted this one to be discovered after my death, but here you are. It's yours. Burn it. Blow it up. Hang it in The State Museum." He returned and handed it to The Mourner.

"I don't know what to say. I'm underwhelmed. This is very bad."

"I call it 'Rodent Holding Candle Against Yellow Background.' You'll notice that the perspective is completely wrong, and that both of the animal's legs are attached to the right side of its body. I'm very proud of this effect, as I am of the light rays projecting from the candle flame. Do you imagine that this will be recognized as Great Art after my death?"

"Absolutely, though it will take a decade for your talents to be affirmed."

"Are you blind?"

"I don't know what you mean."

"You were hoping that I really would be a Great Artist. You'd like nothing better than to contribute to my Discovery after my death, but you will fail. There's no talent to be discovered. Not a lick of it. Your success depends upon finding my neglected Great Works, but after my death, you will find nothing but Bad Art."

"You underestimate your Undiscovered Talent."

"There's so much here, and so little. I've hidden Velvet Elvises in the walls, Weeping Christs and Dancing Country Cats under the floorboards. You'll come with your Loathsome Critics, and they'll find no redeeming paintings. Not one. You'll fail, and your failure will be remembered after your death."

The Mourner gently put down the rodent painting and removed a pistol from her Little Bleak Bag. Her hands shook as she handed it to The Truly Bad Artist. "You leave me no choice. There is one bullet. Russian Roulette. Your death has been scheduled for this evening."

"Isn't Russian Roulette traditionally a game for two?"

"You will be known as a Certified Schizo after your death. As for your Talent, you *will* be honored. I hope that makes you miserable."

"Then what has become of art? Where are the Michelangelos? The Salvador Dalis?"

"Dead. Their work was honored during the Great Conflagration. You know that as well as I."

"Do you know what Great Art is?"

"Great Art is Death by Slow Torture, The Walking Madness, The Perfect Suicide. Great Art is born under the Undertaker's putty knife."

The Truly Bad Artist returned The Mourner's gun.

"I appreciate the kind words, the concern, the delightful company, but I believe that I still have the right to choose my own method of death."

"What then?"

"Let me show you."

They stood on the roof of The Sleaze, overlooking The Bad Side of Town. A dead pigeon lay not far away, within a pool of brackish rainwater, and above, the enormous neon hotel sign, burned and partially melted from an electrical fire, swayed along failing metal rods in the rising wind.

The Truly Bad Artist stared at the street below and asked, "What do you think of Jumpers?"

"For the most part, they're Foolish Investors." The Mourner stood nearby, and seemed pleased by the view. "It's really not done here. It's a Big City Thing, made popular during The Great Depression, long before The Much Bigger Depression. It's a Coward's Death, not at all fitting for a Truly Bad Artist. You're not planning to be a Jumper, are you? It really wouldn't look good for you."

"Nor for you."

He looked at her, smiled, and said, "I don't plan on dying at all. Great Artists are immortal."

"Don't be foolish. The preparations have been made. We're on a *Schedule.*"

"What do you think of The One True Religion?"

"We were talking about your Tragic Death."

"We *were.* You haven't answered my question."

"I don't question The Church. Why should I? The Lord provides."

"No, you don't question. That's obvious. Do you

think?"

"Of course I think. Don't be insulting. I have *feelings*."

"You do? A Mourner with feelings? That's touching. Perhaps I will report you."

The Mourner took a step closer. "You won't have a chance to do that."

"Will you murder me?"

"Of course not. You *will* commit suicide. If you don't do so voluntarily, you will have an Assisted Suicide. That's not my function, but there are others..."

"There's no need for that."

"I see that you don't enjoy pain. I respect you even less now."

The Truly Bad Artist smiled and asked, "Do you really think that I will be Immortal?"

"Most certainly."

He placed his hand on the Mourner's shoulder. "I'm sorry. Have I been unreasonable?"

"Yes." Her voice softened. "It's your nature." They were silent for a time, watched as a Fire of Suspicious Origins engulfed a Newsmonger's Stand below, and then The Mourner said, "I'm worried."

"What?"

"Society. The Church. Sometimes I *do* question it. I've never told that to anyone."

"Why tell me?"

"I don't know. Perhaps it's because you're different, even for a Truly Bad Artist. You *are* different. *Untouched*. You don't seem to be a product of The Church, of Society." She regained her professionalism, then added, "At any rate, you'll be dead by this evening."

"I really *am* a product of Society. I'm no better than

you."

"Are you sure?"

"I'm positive," he answered, and then he pushed her.

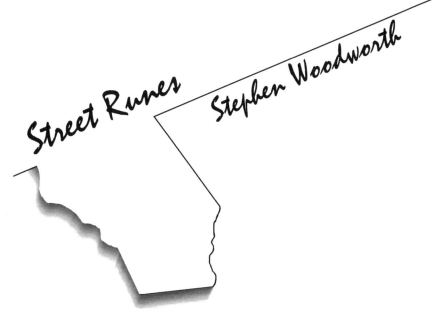

Street Runes — Stephen Woodworth

As Andrea drove to work that morning, she saw that the taggers had struck a house north of Sequoia Avenue.

Almost in reflex, she slowed the Toyota and peered out the dirty driver's-side window at the marked house as if passing a mangled auto wreck. A plump Mexican woman stood on the front walk and complained in frenetic gestures and staccato speech to the white cop beside her, who nodded and took notes on a clipboard. The woman pointed with agitation to the spaghetti-tangled patterns of black spray paint which covered the face of the cottage-style house behind her. Against the pink stucco of the wall, the marks bore a perverse resemblance to tattoos.

They're moving in, Andrea thought as she drove on. This was the first house she'd seen them strike on this side of the freeway overpass which crossed Harper Boulevard. It wouldn't be long before they grew bold enough to invade the upscale neighborhoods north of Longview.

As she pulled into the teachers' parking lot at Morrison High, she wondered if any of her students were involved, but quickly suppressed the idea. She found it hard enough to maintain her enthusiasm without suspecting all her kids of delinquency.

Clusters of teenagers loitered on the concrete walkways between the rows of classrooms. The girls struck poses of supermodel insouciance as hormonal young males clowned and competed for their attention. Some of the boys wore their baggy pants low around their hips, which elongated their torsos and stunted their legs until they looked like the distorted figures from carnival mirrors. Andrea saw several of the kids hide their lit cigarettes as she approached them, but she pretended not to notice – she needed to save her disciplinary energy for later in the day. Mocking smiles on their faces, they whispered to each other in conspiratorial mirth as she passed by. Clutching her file folders to her chest, she kept her gaze downcast until she entered the sanctuary of the faculty lounge.

"– the hell am I supposed to do? Hold back the entire ninth grade?" Brent Waller, the English department chairman, complained as she stepped through the door. Curt Martin, the chemistry teacher, shrugged and took a swig of coffee from his I ♥ FRIDAYS mug. "Hey, that's what the curve is for. If I flunked all the ones who deserved it, my class size would double every semester."

Not wanting to get drawn into the discussion, Andrea headed straight for the copy machine to run off some worksheets.

"Hell, I'd send the seniors back to grade school if I could," Waller went on, running a hand through his collar-length gray hair. "These kids should be reading *Dick and Jane*, not *Romeo and Juliet*."

"Oh, well. Nothing a few thousand dollars of computer equipment can't fix." Martin flashed a taut grin. His eyes pivoted toward Andrea, the slate gray irises peering out from the sagging draperies of his eyelids. "But hey – young turks like Andie here are gonna drum some knowledge into these kids. Isn't that right, Andie?"

"Or die trying." She gave a smile which felt more like a grimace, grabbed the stack of worksheets which had accumulated in the copier's out basket, and left the lounge without even retrieving her original from the machine.

She hated being called "Andie."

A bank of lemon-yellow lockers along one wall of the English Department bore a meaningless squiggle of black paint similar to the one on the house she'd driven past that morning. It had been there almost a month now, for the janitorial staff had tired of painting over the marks which inevitably reappeared within days after the most recent lemon-yellow coat had dried. Andrea shook her head, more out of puzzlement than disapproval. What was it supposed to mean? If it said "School Sucks" or "Metallica Rules" or even "Fuck You," it would at least make sense. Instead, it looked like the crayon scribble of a frustrated four-year-old. The thought that these kids couldn't even write well enough to vandalize properly depressed her further, and she succumbed to an increasing sense of futility as she floundered through her first five classes.

A late September heat wave had descended on Southern California, and the air in the classroom was thick and stagnant. Her sixth-period students slouched in their seats, too listless even to talk amongst themselves. Sweat collected in the small of her back, and the loose fabric of her dress clung to her skin as she stretched to write on the top of the blackboard.

"Now that we know how to separate subjects and predicates, can anyone tell me what the dividing point is in this example?" Andrea asked in a tone of strained cheerfulness, pointing with her chalk to the sentence she'd just scrawled.

They looked back at her with the unseeing eyes of beached fish, the dulled gaze of dying brains. No one spoke a word.

Scanning the rows of blank faces, she saw Luis at the back of the room, slumped over his desk and doodling in a ragged spiral notebook. He'd been one of her favorite students ever since she'd read "The Tell-Tale Heart" aloud in class at the beginning of the year. Luis did an amazing sketch which depicted the narrator burying the old man's dismembered body under the floorboards with the glistening heart looming large in the background. It was morbid, but at least it proved that he'd actually listened to her. The fact that he wasn't paying the slightest attention to her now focused the irritation she felt toward the whole class, and she directed her vexation at him.

"Luis, can you read this sentence and tell us its subject and predicate?"

He sat up and blinked at her as if waking from a doze. "Huh?"

A ripple of laughter ran through the room.

Andrea stalked back to Luis's desk and attempted to snatch the notebook away from him. In a sudden panic, he crossed his arms over the notebook and held it fast to the desktop. "No, Ms. Thomas!"

Her jaw tightened. "Let me see," she commanded.

Luis regarded her for a moment with large brown eyes which were quick and liquid, then took his hands off the notebook and slumped back in his chair with a defeated look.

There on the dog-eared, college-ruled paper was a curlicued snarl of heavy black lines, traced in ink with calligraphic care.

The figure's resemblance to the graffiti Andrea had seen on the house rekindled her suspicion that her own students might be the vandals. Her annoyance with Luis deepened into a sense of betrayal, and she ripped the page out of the notebook and crumpled it in front of his face. "Don't you ever waste class time on this crap again! You understand?"

He nodded, mute.

She threw the wadded paper into the wastebasket by her desk in disgust, then returned to the chalkboard. "Since no one seems to know how to divide this sentence, I guess I'll have to start from the beginning..."

She ended the class with the threat of a pop quiz later in the week, and spent the rest of the afternoon in a sour mood. Though she headed home with a six-inch stack of papers to grade, she seriously considered blowing off the chore that night and drowning her sorrows in white wine and *Seinfeld*.

The marks marring the house on Harper had blackened like dried scabs in the smog-stained sunlight of late afternoon. They tugged at Andrea's peripheral vision as she drove past.

She abruptly stomped on the brake.

Rolling down the window, she squinted at the squiggle spray-painted on the house's front door. A large loop rose from the central tangle of lines, rather like the top of a cursive "S," while two matching spirals curled at the base of the figure.

With an inexplicable sense of urgency, Andrea hung a U and headed back to Morrison.

When she returned to the English department, she saw the janitor's cart parked two doors down from hers and knew she was probably too late. Nevertheless, she dug her keys out of her purse, let herself into her classroom, and rushed over to the wastebasket.

It was empty.

Disappointment mingled with relief. The familiarity of the graffiti on the house gnawed at her, and now she'd never know if her suspicions were correct. Unless...

She stepped back outside and looked toward the janitor's cart. A large trash can lined with a plastic bag sat on its front end.

With a self-conscious glance to either side to make sure no one was watching, Andrea approached the cart and peered into the can. Wrinkling her nose, she gingerly nudged aside some crumpled Taco Bell wrappers and a leaking soft drink cup to see if she could spot a wad of notebook paper somewhere amidst the mass of discarded photocopies at the bottom of the can.

"Help you with something, Miss Thomas?"

Andrea flushed as she lifted her head from the garbage can to see the elderly janitor grinning at her. "Oh,

I'm sorry, Alvin. I... thought I'd thrown away a student's paper by mistake. I was hoping it might still be here."

"Well, go ahead and look all you want," he urged, an amiable North Carolina twang to his voice. He bowed and gestured to the can with one grimy hand. "My trash is your trash!"

She chuckled and thanked him, and Alvin obligingly dumped the can's contents on the pavement for her. A tightly crushed ball of notebook paper rolled out and came to rest on one side of the heap.

She took the ball and picked at its tucked edges until it unfurled.

"That it?" Alvin asked.

Her heart sank as she stared at the figure on the crinkled sheet. A knot of twisted lines with a loop like the top of a cursive "S" and two matching spiral tails. "Yeah, this is it."

Andrea looked forward to sixth period the following day with both impatience and dread. She didn't want to risk alienating Luis, the only student with whom she'd established a real connection, but if he was involved in a gang, she felt obliged to confront him about it before he ended up dead or in jail.

The bell rang to end class, and the students crowded toward the door. While the rest of the kids chattered to each other, Luis lagged alone and silent at the back of the bunch, clasping his dog-eared notebook to his side. As with most adolescent outcasts, a small circle of isolation seemed to surround him.

Andrea positioned herself in the battered wooden office chair behind her desk, fixing her gaze upon him until he happened to make eye contact. "Luis, I want you to stay after for a few minutes."

The end-of-class chatter dropped three decibels, and the empty circle around Luis widened. "I gotta go, Miz Thomas," he pleaded, his feet shuffling as if ready to leave without him. "I gotta help my mama."

"It'll only take a few minutes. Have a seat." She indicated the small chair beside hers, which the kids called "the Deep Shit Seat."

Chewing on his upper lip, Luis trudged to the chair and sagged onto it.

Andrea waited for the rest of the class to exit before speaking. "First of all, I want to apologize for tearing that page out of your notebook the other day. I shouldn't have done that."

Luis didn't respond.

She opened the top drawer of her desk and pulled out the rumpled sheet of paper, now pressed and smoothed to the texture of shed snakeskin. "I like this design," she said, pointing to the cursive pattern on the page. "How did you come up with it?"

He remained as immobile as a mannequin, his eyes focused inward.

"I saw one just like it on a house the other day. What does it mean?"

His gaze shifted abruptly, but not toward her. Instead, he peered out the open classroom doorway. Andrea went to the door to see what had caught his attention.

Outside, two of her "problem children" leaned against the opposite wall, watching her classroom. A failed senior with spiky bleached hair, Eric was merely killing time until his eighteenth birthday freed him from school and unleashed him on society at large. Beside him stood Miguel, a short, quick-tempered Chicano. His biceps ringed with tattoos of barbed wire, Miguel compensated for his lack of height with bodybuilding and machismo. Together, they looked like L.A.'s answer to Laurel and Hardy. She scowled at them and kicked up the doorstop. As the door eased shut, cutting them off from view, she saw Eric point at her and whisper in Miguel's ear.

Andrea turned back to Luis, who waited with the resigned dejection of a dog expecting punishment. "Are they part of your gang?" she asked.

He shook his head, and his mouth opened as if he wanted to correct her, but he didn't speak.

"Come on, level with me! What is this?" She thrust the drawing in front of his face.

He shrugged. "Nothing."

"What does it mean?"

"Nothing! Okay? It don't mean nothing! I just made it up."

"*Doesn't* mean *anything*. And if you made it up, then you put it on that house." She cast the paper aside and reached for the phone on her desk. "I'm going to have to tell your parents about this."

"Mamacita! No!" Dropping his prized notebook, Luis leapt from his chair and seized hold of her hand, pushing the receiver back into its cradle. "You can't!"

Andrea felt his hands trembling as they touched her, and she let go of the phone. She glanced from his pleading face to the notebook, which had fallen open on the floor.

Its pages teemed with ornate, incomprehensible designs.

She stooped to pick it up, but he snatched it and hugged it to his chest.

Placing a hand on his shoulder, Andrea knelt until the two of them were eye-level. "Luis, I want to help. But if you won't let me, I'm going to have to call your mother."

He considered the alternatives a moment, and his expression turned sly. "You won't tell nobody, will you?"

"Anybody." She shook her head. "No."

"If anybody asks, we talked about that test I flunked last week, okay?"

"Whatever you say." She lowered her hand to the notebook, gently prying it away from his chest. "May I see?"

He grudgingly lowered his arms. Andrea surveyed the web of intersecting curlicues on the open page, different from the one she'd seen before. "What is this? Is this your gang's symbol?"

Luis actually laughed at that. "Nah. It's a sentence."

Andrea's scalp prickled. "I don't understand ..."

"See?" Luis pointed to a twist on the upper right side of the figure, then zigzagged his finger from loop to curl throughout the design as he translated.

"'The... time... of... the... New... Lord... has... come.' Betcha can't divide that sentence, can you, Miz Thomas?" He gave a condescending little snicker.

Andrea frowned as she retraced the path his finger had drawn through the maze of lines. "Luis, this isn't funny."

"No, really! That's what it says. Here, look – " He flipped a few pages, then held the open notebook out for her to see. "I started to rewrite that story we read

– the one about the guy who gets walled up in the cellar. Pretty cool, huh?" He grinned with pride.

The page he displayed was nearly black with ink, the interlocking lacework of lines so dense that it gave the sheet the texture of parchment.

"I didn't know a lot of the words, so I had to make some stuff up," Luis explained. "Like the name of that wine."

"Amontillado," she murmured absently, squinting at the drawing as though it were an eyechart which refused to come into focus. "Where did you learn to... write like this?"

"From Him." Luis pointed to the crumpled sheet on her desk.

Andrea shivered as she looked again at the symbol. "Who is 'he'?"

"The New Lord." Luis indicated the paper. "That's His Name. He don't let us say it, though."

"Who is 'us'?" she asked, her own grammar faltering.

"You know – everybody." He swept his hand toward all the empty desks where her students sat.

"But your mom doesn't know about this..."

Luis shifted in his chair. "No. He don't like us to tell nobody like mothers and teachers and shit. That's why you gotta swear not to tell nobody. They'd hurt Mama if she knew." His face darkened. "They'd hurt you, too."

"I see." Andrea folded her hands so Luis wouldn't see them quiver. "I'll promise that, if you promise to stop spray-painting people's houses. Deal?"

The boy mulled over the proposition. "Okay."

"All right, then. You may go now."

Notebook in hand, Luis moved to leave, but paused at the door. "Miz Thomas?"

"Hmm?"

"Could we do some more of that Poe guy?"

She gave him a slight smile. "Sure. If you want."

He allowed her a brief glimpse of his big front teeth in return and opened the door. Sticking his head out like a wary tortoise, he scanned the exterior walkway before stepping outside. As the door clicked shut behind him, a breeze blew across Andrea's desk, rustling the Name of the New Lord.

She was about to ball up the rumpled sheet and throw it back into the trash, but, nagged by a intuitive unease, set it to one side of her desk. As she graded a stack of worksheets she'd collected earlier that day, she glanced back from time to time at the labyrinthine figure on the parchment-like page and shook her head. A new language? These kids couldn't even spell plain English, much less some script which made Arabic seem simple by comparison. Luis's imagination had turned gang vandalism into a secret culture.

Still, even as she lay in bed that night, Andrea couldn't keep the images of Luis's strange script out of her head. Above her, the stuccoed ceiling resembled a page of manic Braille, its patterns pulsing with indecipherable intelligence.

She didn't sleep much that night.

The following morning on her way to work, she almost rear-ended the car in front of her when she nodded off while waiting at a stoplight. Her eyes felt swollen and sticky, and every time she blinked, the promise of cool unconsciousness washed over her. She downed three cups of sludgy coffee in the faculty lounge to try to wake up, and the caffeine made her gaze quiver and her stomach constrict.

The day's first five periods crept past with narcotic monotony. Listless in the stifling atmosphere of the classroom's bottled air, Andrea droned through her lessons on auto-pilot. Fanning themselves with folded worksheets, the students watched her with all the comprehension of monkeys in a zoo. Or maybe she was the monkey, gibbering pointlessly while they regarded her pathetic attempts to communicate with amused contempt.

As she scrawled on the chalkboard, Andrea heard a couple of the girls giggle behind her.

"All right, that's enough," she snapped, turning to face the roomful of smirking faces. "Open your literature books to the story called 'The Lottery,' which you should all have read by now..."

Surveying the room, Andrea spotted a note which was working its way to the rear of the class. When it got to the last row, Josie, the resident fashion-plate, actually put down her nail file for a moment to slide the slip of paper onto Luis's desk. Luis tensed in his chair as he glanced down at the note. The whites of his eyes grew large, and his nut-brown skin appeared to pale three shades.

"Ah! Let's see what we have here." Andrea stalked forward and seized the slip. It was a page ripped from the literature book, its text obscured by a twisted figure which someone had superimposed on the script with a thick black marker.

"All right! What's this supposed to mean?" she demanded, displaying the page.

The class erupted in laughter. Luis was the only

one to remain silent. He sat frozen in the chair, mo-
tionless except for a tiny tremor which ran through his
bony frame.

"I'm not kidding! I want to know who did this."

The laughter swelled, and Andrea's voice cracked
as she shouted over the din. "Okay, that's it! Everyone
turn in your books right now! When I find out where
this page came from, one of you is gonna spend a week
in detention!"

She stood watch as the students filed past and tossed
their copies of the text onto a haphazard pile on her
desk. Eric, she noticed, lagged at the back of the line,
and when the bell rang to end sixth period, he headed
straight for the door.

She moved to block his exit. "Where's yours?"

He shrugged. "I lost it."

"Find it. By tomorrow."

He leaned forward, emphasizing the difference in
height between them, and challenged her with cold, flat
eyes. "Or what?"

Instinctively, Andrea took a step backward. The
reality of his towering figure and broad shoulders fully
impressed itself upon her for the first time. This wasn't
a schoolchild standing in front of her, she realized – it
was a seventeen-year-old man, a foot taller and sixty
pounds heavier than she was. During the day, she could
send him to the vice principal's office, maybe even make
him stay after school and copy definitions out of the
dictionary. But what about at night, on the streets?
What power did she have over him then?

She fought to keep her gaze and voice steady, but
both betrayed her anxiety. "Just find it. Or else."

Eric stretched his thin lips into an icy smirk. "Yeah.

Sure."

He shouldered his way past her and left the room. She saw him glance back and grin at her as he walked away, as though he knew she was watching him.

Andrea let out her pent-up breath and looked down at the crumpled page in her hand. *Much madness is divinest sense...* The rest of Emily Dickinson's words had been buried by the crisscrossing web of the black glyph.

"Luis, do you know what this means...?" She held the figure up for him to see, but found herself alone in the room.

She stayed after school for more than two hours, a vague apprehension making her reluctant to leave the shelter of the classroom. She first went through all the literature books heaped on her desk to see if she could find the one which was missing a page of Emily Dickinson. While the incriminating text never turned up, she discovered to her dismay that pages of nearly every book bore the same sort of infantile scribbling, defaced with pens, pencils, even crayons.

Disheartened, Andrea graded papers in a desultory manner until Alvin poked his head into the room for the fifth time to see if he could come in and clean. Finally getting the hint that it was time to go home, she collected her work, told Alvin the trash was his for the taking, then headed out to the parking lot.

There, just a few yards from her Toyota, lay Luis's notebook, its pages ruffling in the wind like the splayed feathers of a dead bird.

Andrea glanced around the deserted parking lot in a sudden panic, as if she had found Luis's severed hand lying there on the asphalt instead. Miguel and Eric must have really frightened him to make him drop his artwork, she thought, as she stooped and picked up the notebook. Well, she'd put some fear into those boys tomorrow.

She idly flipped through Luis's drawings and rococo designs, smiling when she came across the "Tell-Tale Heart" illustration. The other sketches, all done with a black ball-point pen, were equally macabre: a wolf-headed demon raking a naked woman's body with talons shaped like switchblades; a swarm of gnomes gleefully piercing an emaciated junkie with dozens of syringe needles; a gaseous wraith swooping over a cityscape, trailing a cloud of contamination that blotted out the sun. Above the heads of each of these figures rose comic strip balloons which held more of those cryptic scribbles, some punctuated with the inverted exclamation points used in Spanish.

Andrea shook her head, her smile gone. Poor kid must've been abused to wind up with such a morbid imagination. No wonder the violence of street gangs attracted him.

As she thumbed past sections filled with incomprehensible scribbles, the notebook, as if by habit, opened to a central illustration of a looming, hooded figure. Luis had painstakingly filled in the entire cloak of its body with black ink save for the eyes, which were a vacant white. The figure stood before what appeared to be an old Spanish church or mission whose walls were tapestried with ornate graffiti, and at the spectre's feet a mass of tiny supplicants raised their arms in adulation.

Brainwashing, she told herself, her scalp prickling. Worship the gang leader as though he's a god. Wasn't that how all cults worked? They probably even had their own rituals, their own initiation, their own catechism.

Their own language.

The picture crystallized the concern she'd felt for Luis all afternoon, and almost without realizing, Andrea turned around and headed back to her classroom, her stride quickening to a run.

Once inside the room, Andrea hurriedly flipped open the grade book on her desk and scanned her student list as she picked up the phone. She dialed 9 to get out of the school's system, then punched in the number she'd recorded beside Luis's name on her roll sheet.

The phone at the other end rang six times, giving Andrea ample time to feel like an idiot for calling and to consider hanging up before anyone could answer. She held on, however, until a gruff male voice came on the line. *"Bueno."*

Andrea's mouth hung open, and she felt her face flush. "Um – is Luis there?"

"¿Que? ¿Luis? ¿Quien es?" The voice sounded suspicious.

Andrea hastily attempted to stitch together a few fragments of the high school Spanish she could remember.

"Soy... uh... *maestra.* Ms. Tanner. *¿Está Luis?"*

Andrea evidently convinced the voice that she knew the language, for it rattled off a rapid series of questions, then waited for her reply. She understood maybe one word out of five, tops. *"¡Lo siento – lo siento!"* She hung up the receiver and covered her burning face with her hands.

That went well, she thought with a sigh. What next? Call the police? And tell them what? "I think one of my students is in trouble, officer. I don't know where he is or what he's doing, but he likes to draw disgusting pictures. Look into it, won't you?" The only real evidence she had that Luis was in any actual danger was the fact that he'd dropped his prized notebook. With no more than that to go on, she'd done about all she could do. Sorry, Luis, but you're on your own now, kid.

God, she was beginning to sound like Curt Martin. There had to be *something* else she could do. If only she could give the police some real information about the gang – who was involved, what they did, where they hung out...

Prompted by a dim recollection, Andrea snatched up the notebook and pawed through it to the picture of the robed figure and its adoring congregation. She scrutinized the background behind the ominous form, the building with its Spanish-mission architecture and graffiti-covered walls. The cupola on its roof displayed a pock-marked clock face with Roman numerals. The hands of the clock stood at twenty past ten.

She knew this place. It was the abandoned San Martin train station in the old downtown district. A few years back, the city had considered restoring the Thirties-era building and making it part of the Metrorail system, but they ultimately discarded the plan due to the cost of the project and the crime in the surrounding area. The landmark continued to remain vacant and in disrepair. If she could confirm that this was the gang's meeting site, she might have enough information to get the police involved.

The sun was already sinking below the horizon by the time Andrea finally left Morrison. She skipped her usual turnoff toward home and kept heading south on Harper, descending into the underpass which separated the city's newer, more affluent suburbs from its aging urban district. The freeway bridge arched over her like a triumphal gateway, its concrete columns and embankments decorated with a dizzying patchwork of multicolored hieroglyphics.

As the car climbed the incline on the other side of the underpass, the stark change in the surrounding landscape made Andrea feel like she'd just entered a foreign city. Green yards and pleasant houses gave way to gloomy gray facades of brick and cement. Once home to the town's major banks and businesses, the shabby grandeur of these Depression-era buildings now housed thrift stores, cheap hotels, and porn shops. The sidewalks were vacant and the windows were dark.

Andrea rolled up her window and locked her door. The deeper she drove into the downtown area, the more graffiti she saw. Spray-painted snarls adorned each street sign and store front, eclipsing the words they intended to exterminate. In the purple twilight of the city, these symbols seemed to hold the same arcane significance as Chinese characters, Arabic calligraphy, or Celtic runes. They made Andrea think of the time she got lost in Koreatown, where every incomprehensible sign she came across served as a reminder that she was now the stranger, the outsider, the illiterate.

Situated near the heart of the old city, the train station sulked in the center of a vacant lot, surrounded by a chain-link fence. Its fake adobe face gleamed orange in the light of the street's sodium-vapor lamps. Black patches of graffiti spread over the plaster like a creeping cancer. The clock on its cupola had frozen at twenty past ten.

Andrea parked her car across the street and observed the place for several minutes through her passenger-side window, hoping that she might learn enough from there so that she wouldn't have to leave the safety of her locked car. The site remained silent and deserted as the last ambient light began to fade from the sky, and Andrea decided that she would need to take a closer look now before it became too dark.

Before she got out of the car, however, she pawed through her handbag and pulled out the can of mace she'd carried ever since she'd moved to L.A. It wasn't much, but it reassured her nonetheless.

After only a few minutes of searching, she found a place where the skirt of the fence had been peeled back to allow passage underneath. She obviously wasn't the first person to trespass on this property. As she crouched to pass through the opening, though, a disturbing thought occurred to her: if this was the only way in or out, she could easily become trapped.

Shivering, Andrea stood and surveyed the vacant lot, a rectangular patch of hard-packed dirt littered with beer cans, fast-food wrappers, and a few scattered weeds. The fence bordered the entire lot, then disappeared from view behind the train station. While she couldn't see another opening from where she stood, she figured a gang the size of Luis's would have a wider entrance hidden somewhere.

If the gang existed. If she could find the actual location Luis drew in his notebook, that would be proof enough for her. Then she could get the hell out of there and leave the rest to the cops.

Turning her attention toward the station, Andrea guessed that the mural shown in Luis's drawing must be on the rear wall, out of sight of patrolling police cars.

She tightened her grip on the mace can and edged her way around the building.

Luis's black ink sketch could not have prepared Andrea for what she found on the rear wall. A collision of labyrinthine characters exploded across a plaster surface thirty feet high and fifty feet across, covering the boarded windows and chained doors in that side of the building as well. Overlapping twists and filigrees of glaring red and gold and orange meshed into a fresco of frustrated fury, a visual rendering of the animal howl of ignorance. Branded in black on the center of the mural, the now-familiar Name of the New Lord was the eye of cold calm around which the chaos swirled.

Even in the growing darkness, the artwork appeared to possess a stroboscopic phosporescence, creating the illusion that its intertwining lines shifted and writhed like snakes. Transfixed, Andrea almost failed to hear the murmur of approaching voices, the shifting of gravel beneath many, many feet.

Retreating into the shadows at the side of the building, Andrea peered around the corner at the crowd of silhouettes which advanced toward the station along the rail bed. They followed the tracks up to the broad platform beneath the mural, and as they drew closer, Andrea recognized several of her students.

But there were many more whom she had never seen. Hundreds more.

All teenaged boys and girls, they clustered into a semicircle around the mural as if awaiting a pronouncement. Having seen more than enough, Andrea was ready to run to her car and drive to the nearest police station.

Then they brought out Luis.

Two burly boys, one of whom she recognized as Miguel, dragged Luis into the center of the gathering and forced him to his knees as he writhed and kicked and let out a strange keening shriek. Andrea next saw Eric emerge from the crowd of spectators to inspect the prisoner. In his right hand, Eric held a can of spray paint, idly shaking it as he circled around Luis, grinning.

The crowd grew quiet, and Luis's shriek diminished to a whimper. For a moment, all Andrea could hear was the rhythmic clacking of the paint can. Then Eric lifted the can over his head and shouted a series of sneering nonsense syllables to which the crowd responded with whoops and whistles.

As they cheered him on, Eric leaned toward Luis and sprayed black paint into both of the smaller boy's eyes. He added a black slash across the mouth, a perverse clown's grin, turning Luis's visage into an ironic smiley face. Miguel dug his fingers into Luis's side to make him scream so that Eric could shoot paint into the boy's open mouth, coating his tongue and teeth.

"STOP!" Startled by the volume of her own voice, Andrea stepped out of hiding to confront the suddenly silent gathering. She knew she didn't stand a chance against all of them, but she had to do something to keep them from killing Luis. With the can of mace held out at arm's length as though it were a .38 Special, she moved toward Eric and Luis's other captors. "Get away from him," she commanded.

Eric grinned, then nodded at Miguel and the other boy. They let go of Luis, who dropped onto the cement, his painted mouth bobbing open in a rasping, asthmatic gasp.

Struggling to mask her fear with cool authority, Andrea surveyed the multitude of mute, impassive faces which regarded her. "I already called the police," she lied. "They should be here any second."

No one moved to threaten her, and Andrea briefly wondered if her bluff had actually worked. Her hope evaporated as a torrent of laughter rolled through the crowd. It was just like in the classroom, she realized, angry tears welling in her eyes. Only now they didn't have to wait until she turned her back to jeer at her.

Still, none of them tried to attack her. Instead, they began to chant a succession of discordant, slurred squeals and clicks and screeches, like the chattering of a locust swarm. At first, the din sounded as formless as white noise, the verbal equivalent of radio static, but as the teens' voices rose in chorus, Andrea discerned a pattern in their vocalizations, a mantra.

An invocation.

Andrea dropped the can of mace and clamped her hands over her ears. Their alien tongue sent surges of visceral nausea throughout her body, as if the grating of chalk against a blackboard had been amplified a hundred million times. And as she stared aghast at the rapture on their faces, Andrea understood that they had been waiting for her to join them. Indeed, Eric and Miguel must have left Luis's notebook in the school parking lot as her invitation to the mass.

Tonight, she would receive her education. Tonight, she would learn the language of the New Lord.

Its alphabet was born of shattered windows, cracked pavement, and tangled freeways. Its speech was the cacophony of car horns, sirens, and gunshots. It offered hope of a higher intelligence to children left half-sentient by a society which had allowed its own language to wither with disuse.

And, like every language which preceded it, it had fostered its own deity.

A sudden glare bathed the chanting congregation in bluish-white light, and Andrea turned to see what had caused it. She found that the ebony symbol in the center of the mural now shone with a luminescence which seemed to emanate from deep within the wall.

Sinking to her knees, Andrea quoted the Bible in her mind: *In the beginning was the Word, and the Word was with God, and the Word was God.*

A black mist billowed from the glowing insignia on the wall before her.

And the Word was made flesh.

Andrea didn't notice when dawn came.

Hours passed uncounted in the deserted classroom, the silence broken only by the hum of fluorescent ceiling panels and the whisper of chalk on slate. Andrea scrawled each slash and swirl as if by rote, as though she were copying definitions from a dictionary. Oblivious to the numbness of her legs and the stink of her sweat-stained blouse, she didn't stop even when she heard the door open behind her.

"Andrea? You're here early." Brent Waller's voice. "I saw your light on and wanted to make sure – What the hell is *that?*"

She paused in mid-stroke and cast a pitying glance at the bewildered expression of the English department chairman, who stared, uncomprehending, at the anarchy of lines which covered the entire chalkboard. She smiled, but didn't speak. He wouldn't have understood her, anyway. There was much he didn't understand.

But he would learn. Soon, they all would.

School was now in session.

A Flock of Drunk Witches

Dana Vander Els

"My cousin's half-sister's uncle is in a band."

Liz took a swig of her birthday bottle of Olde English 800, belched self-consciously, and said, "Yeah, yeah. My ex-boyfriend back in Cerritos was a roadie for Goldenvoice, and he's twenty-two."

The sun wove pleasant patterns in the branches over the dugout cellar hole. Liz thought about Jeff, her new crush, and decided he was a fucking asshole anyway.

"So? Then he's like, a child molester," said Tina "If you did anything. Anyway, my cousin's whatever is in a band, and they can't play, either. I mean, they learned, really fast, you know, 'cause they were playing parties and stuff."

"He wasn't a child molester! Even if we did anything. Rudy told me a really cool name for our band: A Flock of Drunk Witches. We could have t-shirts that say, 'Kill the bitches' on the front and 'A Flock of Drunk Witches' on the back."

Dolores yawned. "Did we smoke all the pot yet?"

"No," Letty said. It was the first thing out of her mouth in at least an hour. Liz wasn't sure she liked her, not because she smoked heroin and was a total slut, but because she could never figure out whether her silence and general sullen attitude concealed extreme intelligence or extreme stupidity. Liz also had no idea why she was at her runaway birthday party, but she'd brought wine.

Tina handed Liz their first score with reverence, another present, and Liz rolled it like she meant it. She lit the spliff with a flourish and passed it to Tina, even though Dolores was all ready to take it.

"Good thing you got that can of Bugler," Tina said. "You going to be okay out here? All the trippy shit on the walls..." She waved the burning joint at the series of spirals and pentagrams drawn in chalk on the gray stones of the drywall foundation.

"This place is like, I dunno, really spooky," Dolores said. "Don't bogart it – give it to me."

"Yeah, what if this is the Nightstalker's secret hideout?" said Letty, breaking all records for conversation with other chicks. Here they were in the foothills, and Letty was wearing fishnets and a leather bra. This was fucking John Muir and mountains, not the Olympic Auditorium. Only Tina got it.

"Oh, the Nightstalker. He doesn't kill people out in the woods."

But he had killed in their town. Two little old ladies right up the street from the Mormons, the foster home she'd run away from a week ago. It was scary shit, the Nightstalker right in Monrovia, a cute, old town that had seemed so safe compared to Norwalk and the one-ways.

"Stop it, you guys. You're freaking me out," she whined in the Anika voice from Pippi Longstocking. Tina and Dolores giggled. Their only song was called "Anika Grew Up To Be A Junkie," and Liz was the author. Letty just stared at the dark blue sky.

The light danced low in the canyon. Liz thought hazily of the damned benignity of it all. She had the "Complete Works" of Arthur Rimbaud in her backpack, and pitched forward to get it out and perfect her mood. She picked up her Olde English, but it was killed. Dolores and Tina woke up from their trance like a game of poker, got up, and stretched.

Dolores started agitating to take off, and the other girls' buzzes had evaporated enough to make it sound good. Liz felt the mood and was cool with it. She and Arthur and John Muir and the San Gabriels, all alone. That was visceral living.

"You can stay in my garage tomorrow," Tina said, and squeezed her shoulder. Liz smiled up at her plain brown face. "Yeah, that'll be cool."

The three girls collected their stuff and waved goodbye. Romantic derelict stone stairs lead past the still solid fireplace, where the backpacks and Letty's patent leather purse lay atop a small pile of branches she'd collected with Tina. They came to the abandoned dugout a lot, and Liz got the idea of spending her birthday alone in the woods. Hikers used the cabin. It was her secret with Tina that she might try to live there.

Letty, Dolores, and Tina waved again from the top of the dugout walls. They were out of sight in the thick underbrush in a few moments. The faint ripple of the low creek sounded louder the minute they were gone.

Pushing herself a little, she walked up the stairs with the big wine bottle and the camping skillet to fill at the creek. Dark was on its way. An uneasy sense of being watched flashed in her brain. She shook it away, angry at her urban stupidity. Live oaks marked the watercourse, and despite herself she looked behind her each time she passed one.

The din of the creek once arrived at was remarkable. The afternoon darkened rapidly into twilight, and all at once it was colder. She filled the bottles quickly, numbing her fingers. As she stood up a noise cracked above the noisy water. She froze.

"Okay, so now I'm going to make a fire." The canyon walls felt closer now, and the thought of all that dry chaparral made her nervous. The fire place looked fine, even used recently, but she took extra care lighting it.

She dropped two packages of Top Ramen in the skillet of water. Rimbaud stood on his spine, but she just couldn't settle down to read him. She rolled another Bugler and smoked it. She wished she wasn't so fucked up. Sounds came out of nowhere and down in the cellar hole she couldn't see much but the steep sides of the canyon. It was all paranoia, anyway. She stuck a candle in the top of the wine bottle and tried to read, but ended up pacing back and forth; she stirred the barely boiling water and noodles and hovered over the measly fire.

The crashing noise in the brush repeated itself.

Her spine tensed like a whiplash. In an agony she realized she had to pee, really badly. It was probably a deer or coyote; there was a drought and this was the water. She had to piss really bad and it was stupid, being afraid of wild animals, and there were extra branches up there they hadn't bothered to drag down into the dugout. She'd get those and keep the fire burning if it was coyotes, who were afraid of fire, at least in books.

Shaking, she mounted the steps in the deep dusk. The candle cast a noticeable yellow glow down in the stone hole, but the fire, to her dismay, was petering out in her absence. She dragged down her jeans and gulped deeply to make herself pee, but she couldn't go. She tried counting prime numbers. Then she heard the cracking sound again, and the piss streamed out. The hair stood up and prickled on the back of her neck. The chaparral rustled and moved at the top of the steep canyon wall in front of her.

She pulled up her pants, flew to the cabin, jumped down the stairs, dashed the noodles on the smoking fire, tucked her can of Bugler inside her thermal, zipped her jeans, and grabbed the candle. She leaped back up the stairs, and now the crashing sound reverberated and was coming down the slope from three directions in the swaying brush. She heard a fourth behind her, logical from the pattern they formed, coming four-angled into the canyon's narrow upper end.

Liz splashed into the creek. It flowed down and away from the shapes, shrouded figures glimpsed through leaves and branches. A low, resonant caterwauling echoed off the canyon.

In some still place she marveled at the incredible burst of speed she was capable of. Her senses were like calculators computing dozens of linear equations, skipping over slimy rocks and flinging her headlong. On instinct she abandoned the candle in the water as she climbed down the first cement flood-control waterfall, skinning her hands and almost losing a shoe, but doing every calculation in a frenzy, running, running, running, never losing balance, to the next waterfall, the noise of chase and now human voices audible, noticing blood on her hands in the dark without blinking an eye except to wonder if they could smell and track her that way.

Three, four, five flood control gates. Her body flew through the motions of flight. They had flashlights. It was real, it was really happening; her body flung her into the undergrowth itself and found rabbit trails through the poison oak and manzanita and bramble. She crawled like an electroshocked dachshund and ran, panting, on all fours, when the tunnels were tall enough.

She began to stumble. She couldn't hear them and knew she hadn't been able to for a while. She was on an almost vertical bank, with a stone outcrop of the ridgeline to the right. A big twisted bush grew out of cracks in the rock. She ran to it and squatted in its shadow. Her forehead was pounding and sweat shivered off her hair and face as she shook from head to toe. She slowed her breathing to alleviate her cottonmouth.

Liz almost started to think when she saw flashlights at the base of the bank. Her nerves zinged to life and electrical impulses propelled her over the top of the rock cluster. Her nerves shrieked naked joy at the site of the long wide spine of the ridge, and she was off with her burst like a track star. Voices shouted behind her. Male. Human.

The ridgeline was paved with small stones and free of shrubs. She wouldn't look back, and finally her mind started functioning. She was miles from the trailhead that went back down to Tina's house. Folded sides, like concave ribs to the ridge's spine, swept down to the city side. The lights of Monrovia, Arcadia, Duarte, the whole damn basin under a clear sky lay below her. She ran for what felt like hours or minutes. Again, the pursuit died out.

She sat down at the first likely spot and flopped like a rag doll out of simple exhaustion. For a long, long time she stared at the stars and the lights of the whole city, until her neck hairs alerted her. The sensation of being watched and powerlessness to continue overwhelmed her.

Soundless and predatory as an owl, raising its arms like the owl beats soundless wings, a tall, black hooded shape seemed to rise out of the ground a hundred feet down the ridge. Liz gasped. Her body jerked into action, sliding at the rib of the mountain.

She careened down the shale on a broken rollercoaster ride, slashing her hands and face in low branches of cholla, bucketing down, down. The seat of her pants went and she didn't even notice. The rib of stone ended abruptly in a thicket of cactus. She scrambled to her feet and around the near side of the clump. Another brief spine of shale stopped in a stretch of lamplit bushes and agave. There were houses beyond. She ran and fell the final dozen yards of ridge. She fought her way through the crazy growth, branches pulling at her clothing, and then she was in someone's backyard.

The asphalt lay just beyond. She ran toward it,

gripped by the horrifying sense that the house might belong to the hunters. The road curved into blackness, but down, out of the foothills, and she raced to reach populated regions. She had to be safe, surrounded by human beings.

The housing tract road ran into a main artery of Foothill Boulevard. She took it, and ran, all the way down the hill, all the way to Foothill Boulevard, and in the lights and gas stations and fast food joints she found salvation and wept. A bank clock flashed 3:09.

She was near Sierra Madre; she recognized the Falafel Palace. The few cars on the road dragged her and stared. She walked steadily south and down Foothill until she came to a part of town she knew. There was no place to go. She walked farther, until she could go straight back up the hill to Tina's road, if only she could cross the street. A lowrider dragged her, laughing and shouting, "Junkie!" She ignored them. They went away.

Liz stopped in front of a gas station. The light was on inside, and a man was sitting behind the counter. He was fat and seedy-looking, wearing an oily plaid shirt.

He stared as she pushed open the heavy door.

"Let me use your phone."

"I'll call the cops," he warned. He was greasy, pockmarked, fat, and middle-aged. He became terrifying.

"Let me use your fucking phone to call my family! I've been chased down the mountain by satanists! Fucking imbecile! Moron! Let me use the fucking phone!"

He grabbed the telephone and began dialing. Liz cried out hoarsely. He hesitated. She ran.

She collapsed behind the planting of a different gas station. She rolled herself a Bugler. Her thirst had vanished. She smoked and thought of the dawn, the sunlight only a couple hours away.

Across the street, a familiar orange-haired figure moved drunkenly up the street. All in black, like always: Rudy. She called out his name. He veered across the street.

He lit her one of his Camels. The story burst in erratic floods of disjointed description. He put his arm around her. She cried.

"I'm going over to Greg's. He lives in his parents' old garage. They're afraid of him. They'll never notice. I'll take you over there." He smiled his beautiful joker's smile.

Greg's detached stucco garage had a regular door cut into the garage door. He was a weird guy, but he went to Monrovia High; she'd ditched school with him. Greg and Jeff and Mel flopped on paisley couches built of wooden crates, drums and amplifiers and guitars propped against walls. Rudy told them the story in two sentences, and Greg tossed her a can of beer.

"Show her the shower," he told Rudy. Rudy led the way to a tiny bathroom with a camp shower and plywood walls. Rudy gave her a deep, brown-eyed look, and in spite of everything blood rushed to her groin. Rudy quirked one side of his mouth up and walked away. She sighed. The nightmare drained away. Maybe they'd get together.

"She's a little dyke. She's definitely a virgin," she heard Jeff say loudly as she closed the bathroom door. Her face burned. Oh my *God*.

She showered a long time. She discovered her

bruises and hundreds of cuts. Twigs stuck out of hair. She pulled them out. She regretted she had no makeup, not even some base. When she could put it off no longer, she unlocked the door and exited in a cloud of steam.

The guys were waiting for her. Rudy smiled, oh so slow.

"Tape her mouth," said Letty, coming in from the kitchen, "She talks too much." She slid the brush knife in her hand back and forth across the whetstone.

Jeff walked up with the duct tape. In the corner, Tina and Dolores held each other, naked, and rolled their dead eyes at nothing.

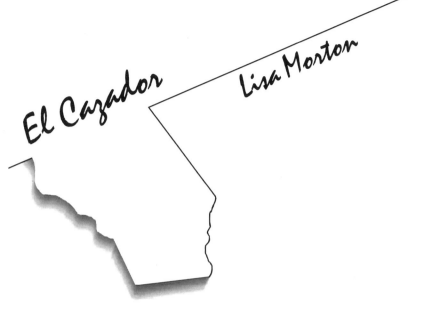

El Cazador

Lisa Morton

This manuscript is not written in blood.

El Cazador's name has already been written enough in that vital ink; if there were colors for sweat and tears he would've found a way to use those as well. No, what you see here is only printer's ink, black and unalive, and so not his art... perhaps more like the artist himself. I can say that because I've known him. I may not know exactly who he is or *how* he became El Cazador, but...

I know *what* he is.

Unfortunately this story starts with me. Not a very good journalistic practice, but then I wasn't a very good journalist. I was a freelancer earning my keep as a waitress, living with two roommates in a two-bedroom apartment and looking for that one big story that would excite some movie producer and get me into the studios. So far I'd sold one article on the origins of molé sauce. It had not become the next *Like Water For Chocolate*.

My interest in El Cazador began with someone else's article in the paper, a short single column buried in the Valley section of a Tuesday morning *Times*. It noted only that the mutilated body of a gang kid had been discovered not far from one of the tags of "El Cazador," a notorious graffiti artist who had frustrated police and citizens' action groups in North Hollywood/Sun Valley for over a year now.

I already knew the name. I remembered seeing it once on an overpass of the 118 Freeway. It was intricate, in red and orange and black, and the three of us in the car at the time had wondered who would have been insane enough to hang from a freeway while traffic sped by below just so they could scrawl their name.

"Scrawl," though, wasn't appropriate. Even while the others were laughing about it I remember thinking it was surprisingly fluid, dynamic. It left its imprint on the mind's eye as if the tagger had personally written it *there*. When I suggested to my friends that there was no real difference between the work of Keith Haring and that of El Cazador they'd scoffed, derided me the rest of the day. But I knew the truth about El Cazador's work.

It was art and it was magnificent.

A year later I saw the newspaper article and within hours I was determined to be El Cazador's definitive chronicler. It was perfect: I would find out what Valley gang he ran with, track him down, get his bio, sell the article, and split the million dollars that Paramount or Columbia would pay us for the film rights.

Of course I was aware of a few little problems with this plan. I was a 26-year-old white female whose grasp of Spanish was – well, not even a fingerhold. I didn't know anything about Hispanic gangs or taggers or that part of the Valley. I knew it could be dangerous, certainly, but I had my pepper spray and a 1980 Plymouth Horizon nobody would want to steal.

I decided to start by driving around, finding whatever I could of El Cazador's work, photographing it and documenting the location. Then I would assemble an album, evidence of my serious interest, and locate him by questioning the locals.

The first part of the plan proved to be easy. El Cazador's work was plentiful and identifying it was as simple as picking a genuine Van Gogh out of a paint-by-numbers collection.

Commencement was the discovery of a mural on the side of a crumbling apartment complex on the northern end of Vineland. It covered the entire side of the ramshackle building, three floors high and two apartments wide. It could be seen from three blocks away, dominating a neighborhood of dented, overflowing garbage cans, ancient bungalows with brown lawns and barred doors, liquor stores with wooden boards over the windows.

The subject was survival, violence: a snake fighting an eagle. The two combatants were locked in a full-on struggle, yet the serpent was clearly winning. Its venomous fangs were buried halfway in the eagle's carefully feathered neck, its sinuous length coiled once around the contorting bird. One of the eagle's wings was nearly torn off and its head was tilted back, beak open, screeching its agony. The snake was grinning.

At the bottom, formed from the shower of avian blood, was the signature "El Cazador."

It was breathstopping, rendered in colors so extravagant I had to remind myself they had all come from mere spray-paint cans. It bespoke careful planning and long nights of exhaustion. It brought associations to mind, pricked the backbrain with unnameable mythologies... and yet the political statement was clear as well.

In the Mexican flag the eagle is winning.

The surrounding space was cluttered with simple black graffiti letters, most in the pointed, sharp style that always appeared vaguely extraterrestrial to me. These lesser tags were layered thick on top of each other, spilling haphazardly, something that might have been "Killahs" across "Felipe Z" covering "IMAW," but no one had touched El Cazador's. Even the lifeless dirt at the base of its wall was clean of the usual rubbish. It was obviously held in veneration.

I had to walk halfway down the block to get it all in my lens. While I was snapping shots a boy, maybe ten, walked up to me. He had dark skin, serious eyes, and a Tecate beer T-shirt.

"You from County?"

"County?"

"Yeah, you know, clean up or somethin'?"

I looked down at him, trying to seem open and friendly. "No, I like the painting."

It succeeded. "Oh, tha's cool. El Caz, he's the best, man."

Could it really be this easy? I asked, "You a friend of his?"

The boy frowned, disappointed. "I wish. Ain't nobody his friend."

"Somebody must be," I nodded at the mural. "He couldn't have done that alone."

"He did, an' in one night."

"One night? No way."

"Yas, man, I'm tellin' you, was one night. See how all the street lights an' shit is broke out?"

I glanced around. He was right – every light in the immediate area was smashed.

"That's so he'd be harder to see while he did it."

I smiled and asked, "Then how'd he see?"

The boy answered, "I dunno. He's El Caz. Me, I only live in the building."

Then he got on a skateboard and rode off.

I watched in disbelief. He wasn't lying – he skated in through the main entrance of the building.

Wait a minute, so maybe he *did* live there, that didn't mean he hadn't lied about the rest. The only way that painting could have been completed in one night would have involved a small army of artists with their own lights and the boy had said El Cazador worked alone. Of course I was still the outsider, the dipshit who could be had for a ridiculous fairy tale. That kid was probably in one of those apartments right now laughing his head off at the stupid chiquita who bought that dumb story, man.

Maybe this wouldn't be so easy after all.

I photographed six more El Cazador tags over the next two weeks. I also clipped three newspaper stories about gang slayings that had occurred not far from the tags.

Pedro Lopez, eighteen, was found a quarter-mile from a Los Angeles river concrete wash on which two gleaming, blocky robots battled it out, red fluid spraying from vents in their silver plating. Pedro's throat had been ripped open. Fourteen-year-old Eduardo Maneiros was found nearly severed in half beneath a warehouse wall displaying an Aztec priest ripping the heart from a pale, shrieking girl. A depiction of a gang shootout with bullets the size of basketballs, painted in an alley, could have been the last thing fifteen-year-old Tony Castro saw before he was slashed repeatedly with a sharp object.

Were El Cazador's paintings inspiring violence? Were these killings morbid homage, sacrifices to the legendary tagger king? Or was it coincidence? There were kids dying everywhere, after all.

The people I talked to in El Cazador's neighborhood couldn't offer much. Most didn't know anything. Some didn't speak English. Several laughed at me. One twentythree-year-old gangsta named Cruz told me nobody knew who El Caz was, he was solo, didn't run with a gang. Then Cruz asked me out. He told me I'd never find El Cazador if I hadn't experienced how he lived. He followed me all the way to my car, then leaned on the hood until I pulled away. I could see him grinning in the rearview mirror. I've had a couple of dreams about Cruz since then. They were bad.

One early morning, a little past eight, I found an old man who spoke only Spanish staring at a fifteen-foot high scene of robocops battering a crouching boy, painted on the back wall of a building housing a hardware store. When he saw me the old man gestured at the wall and the broken lights, rattling off an angry string. I could gather only that the painting was recent and he wasn't too happy about it. When I shook my head apologetically he walked closer to the wall and tapped at the brownish-red letters spelling out "El Cazador."

"Sangre, sangre," he shouted.

I knew that word, at least. Sangre.

Blood.

Then the old man shook his head angrily, murmured "policia" and hobbled back up to the main street and into the tiny panaderia bakery he owned.

I stared at the stylized signature, wondering what he'd meant. Sure, it was the color of dried blood, the implication was there...

What if it wasn't implication?

I touched the wall, brushing my fingertips over the surface. All I felt was the coarse brick and mortar construction. Other tags covered any surface not taken by El Cazador's, but they were scribbled by clumsy, insensitive hands and looked old, ignored.

I scraped at the dark side of one of the detailed assailants. The chromium blue felt sealed, like spray paint. It didn't come off.

When I scraped at the red lettering in the name it was still slightly damp.

A sticky blob came off on my fingertip. I rubbed it against my thumb and it dissolved into something thick and very dark red.

I backed away, staring at my fingers, a nervous thrill in my stomach. The meaning revealed there was obvious. El Cazador, my elusive quarry, was not just a kid with a talent for creative vandalism. This was something darker, something –

I nearly lost my balance as my right foot caught behind me. I glanced down, expecting to be disgusted by dog shit or old newspapers —

— and saw instead a boy, a dead boy, his torso torn open, red and gray matter spilling out. His face was smeared, the ground all around him black and viscid. There was a gun not far from him, lying useless. The fingers of one hand still seemed to be clawing for it. The flies had already settled on him.

What I did next... usually people say they felt sick, they felt weak, they screamed.

I took a picture.

Then I turned and ran for my car.

In the paper the next day was a back-page item about another gang slaying that had evidently taken place less than a block from one of El Cazador's tags. This time his name was mentioned, but police were uncertain whether a connection "can be absolutely drawn to the graffiti artist." They were also seeking a possible witness, "a woman, white, blonde hair, early twenties, carrying a camera."

I would give it up, this story. It should ideally be written in a language I didn't speak. A language in which "sangre" meant a color in the arsenal of a tagger.

I would go back to my life, my world. I would write articles on schoolkids who get to interview the president, on cats who could mouth the word "hello" and whether herbal remedies actually helped or not. Eventually, perhaps, I might write a screenplay. A gentle romantic comedy. A coming-of-age drama. Anything without images of boys, ripped apart, dying beneath murals painted in passion and blood.

I wish I could say it was a dream or a vision that

changed my mind, that I was obsessed, driven, that I had an unquenchable curiosity or thirst for knowledge.

But it was simple, stupid, anger, of the righteous type.

It was a bit on a local weekly television news show about a group called **CANT** – **C**itizens **A**gainst **N**eighborhood **T**agging. They were mainly white, lower-middle class, male. El Cazador had recreated a grisly, fatal traffic accident on a brick wall near a treacherous intersection. The members of **CANT** busily blanketed the wall, regardless of the fact that the brick was red and their paint wasn't. Gray rolled over the face of a woman, screaming above the body of a boy. Gray covered a car in which the chrome was so intricate you could imagine the owner polishing it on a Sunday afternoon. Gray overspread the vivid crimson splashes of El Cazador's signature.

The spokesman for the group said it was "time citizens take a stand against vandalism in their own communities." When asked, he admitted he didn't live anywhere nearby; he did, however, own a real estate firm which held property in the area.

The worst, though, was Henry Colson. Henry was thirtytwo, unemployed, and had joined **CANT** because it was "high time somebody stood up for the right to live in a clean, decent neighborhood free of scum." Henry said he advocated "whatever methods necessary." By the time he got to the part about "welfare children who can't even speak the language of the country that's supporting them," he had gone on so long without pause that they had to cut away from him in mid-sentence.

El Cazador was possibly dangerous, but it was a danger that represented mystery, fire, heart and soul. He wanted to decorate his world in shades of red, shades that disturbed, true, but that also provoked, inspired, and enlivened. These others would protect their territories by pissing gray in all the corners.

I knew now I had to write this. I couldn't let El Cazador be buried by the people who wanted us all to live in their soft shades of ash. I would have to find him. I would have to accept the risk of becoming the palette for his name.

Several weeks later, weeks of fruitless driving, unanswered or misunderstood questions, fearful encounters, shameful encounters...

...I found the unfinished one.

At first I didn't know it for what it was. I knew only that it was different from the rest.

The area was an industrial nightmare, partly abandoned foundries, boarded-up warehouses, parking lots whose asphalt had long since cracked and sprouted ragged sage. I passed few cars and no pedestrians going in or out of the vicinity. The canvas was a concrete freeway support wall; fifty feet overhead traffic rushed, unaware of this rotten underworld. The scene was two half-human demons locked in hand-to-hand combat. Ichor gushed from wounds made by tooth and talon. I could virtually feel the pressure of locked muscles, straining backs, tearing hide. It was nearly thirty feet tall, still twenty-five feet below the freeway. *How does he do it?*, I wondered, not for the first time. The scarlet signature was there, but it trailed off strangely at the lower left corner.

I glanced around, saw I was alone, then got out the camera and started snapping. It was late in the day;

the painting faced west and the low sun was golden. I was framing another angle when I noticed something through the viewfinder: a small white square on the street below the mural. It looked as if it was stuck there by tape or glue.

I lowered the camera and walked up to it. When I realized what it was I felt a treasure hunter's thrill.

It was a rough sketch of the painting above. It had been taped to the wall for reference. It also clearly proved that the bigger work had been left incomplete, because in the lower corner a group of small boys watched the vicious combatants, their expressions both enrapt and afraid. Two of them had broken into their own fight, imitating the main event.

He hadn't had time to finish here. What if it had been last night? What if he might be back tonight to finish it?

I returned to my car and moved it into an empty parking lot, partly hidden by overgrown scrub brush. I moved the seat back for comfort, locked the doors, and settled in.

I would be here when he came.

It was after eleven when the lowrider car appeared, stopped where its headlights splayed out across the mural, three figures inside pounding armrests to the beat of Ice-T.

For some reason I'd never thought about the flesh El Cazador to match the blood. But if I *had* ever stopped to picture him, the boy who got out of the car and studied the unfinished tag would have been image come to life.

I had screwed a 300mm telephoto lens onto the

camera and I used it then to spy on him. Lit by his car's headlights he was no more than eighteen, but already tall, over six feet, well-built. He wore a sleeveless-T revealing muscled, tattooed arms. Handsome, with deep-set eyes and thick, lustrous black hair curling to his neck.

The tattoos on his arms were miniaturized versions of all of El Cazador's tags.

The tattoos, the way he studied the piece with such intensity... it had to be him.

I unlocked the car door, took the photographic album I'd compiled (the *catalogue raisonné*), and, holding the rough sketch before me like a truce flag, approached. He had turned at the sound of the car door opening and watched me, expressionless.

I stopped five feet away. "Is it you?" I asked, nodding at the mural.

He glanced at the sketch, then back at me, smiling. "Maybe."

Suddenly my heart was pounding, my fingers shaking as I held the album up, flipping through the pages for him to see. "I've been documenting your work. I want to write about you, so people can understand what you're doing..."

"What do you think I'm doing?"

I looked into his black eyes and answered, "Putting your soul on display."

He considered, then said, in that accent peculiar to this part of the Valley, "You wanna write 'bout me, huh? So you can make a lotta money, right?"

"Well — sure, I mean we both can. But what I really care about is the work. The *art*. The citizens' action groups think you're nothing but a vandal. They want to whitewash your tags."

"Whitewash, huh? I guess that's somethin' you'd know all about." His eyes flicked behind me. "That your car?"

No, this was wrong. "My car... ?"

"In this neighborhood somebody could steal it." He was advancing on me now, grinning. I started backing away.

Then he called out in Spanish past my shoulder. I jerked around and saw the other two in the car. They were getting out now, moving slow, enjoying this. One walked over and deliberately slouched himself against the driver side door of my car. The third stopped a few feet from me. They both had bottles of bad malt liquor and moist blunts.

I faced the original boy, trying to keep my voice even. "You're not him, are you?"

"Why not?"

"Because he works alone."

He pretended to think that over, then laughed. "Guess you're right, chiquita, because we always do everything together."

The one closest to me, wiry, bad teeth, buzzcut, stepped up to my side. "Bet you never had any _real_ Mexican food, huh, baby?"

"I'm just looking for El Cazador. If you know him you can tell him for me – "

The first one slapped me. Not hard, but enough to leave my face stinging and bring tears to my eyes. "Why the fuck you think El Caz'd wanna talk to _you_?! He's not _yours_, you dumb college bitch. He's _ours_. You even know what his name means?"

Oh christ. All these weeks and it had never even

occurred to me that the name itself meant anything.

"Goddamn, you ain't much of a writer, you didn't even do your homework. El Cazador means 'the hunter.' That's us. That's what we do, like him. We hunt."

"Loco lobos," Bad Teeth giggled.

"We protect our territory. And you strayed into it, little white rabbit – "

I made a break for my passenger door.

I didn't make it. They got me, bent me back on the hood. Bad Teeth was clawing at my shirt while the others held me down, whooping and taunting in half Spanish, half English.

I can't say for sure what happened next.

The gangstas over me were blown apart, like dead leaves in a sudden hurricane. I saw Bad Teeth grappling with someone, then he shouted a hoarse obscenity, a knife blade appeared through his back and blood splattered my legs and the car. Oh god that thick metal smell... Tattoo had a gun out, the third one had his own knife. Whoever – whatever – had hit them went for the knifeholder first. The hand holding the stiletto was suddenly bent backward, little cracks sounding. The knife fell and its former possessor shrieked. The assailant shoved him away and stared at the boy with skin art and gun. "Go, vato! Now!"

Tattoo looked around frantically and realized he was alone now; his friends were either dead or fled. His fingers were shaking as the man with his back to me pointed at the tattoos and said softly, "I let you go 'cause 'a the art, man."

Tattoo stowed the gun, got in his car, gunned the engine and peeled out.

I was crouched on the ground, huddled against the protective metal of a fender. Now the aggressor turned and I saw him by the dim light of overhead freeway traffic.

He was no man. He was young, more so than the others – sixteen at best. Small, skinny, acne-scarred face, stringy unwashed hair.

This couldn't be him.

The Hunter.

"El Cazador..."

The boy with the teeth and the knife in his back moaned and scrabbled at the asphalt. His attacker turned away from me, walked idly over and pulled the knife out of him. Then El Cazador – because this *was* him – knelt beside the twitching boy, flipped him onto his back – and tore his throat out with his teeth.

This was not the polite seduction of a thousand midnight movies. The victim pinned beneath El Cazador was flailing wildly in his last seconds of life. He tore at his killer's hair and clothes, uttered choked babbling cries, bucked his body, tried to dislodge the thing sucking him dry. Blood puddled beneath him and began to run.

I picked myself up and sidled to the passenger door. I'd forgotten it was locked. The keys were in my pocket. I got them out, wrapping my fist around them to stop the jangling noise. The click of the key in the lock, the creak of the door opening sounded like cannonfire to me, but El Cazador paid no attention, still embroiled in his grotesque feast. I slid in and locked both doors. My fingers were shaking as I got the keys into the ignition. I started the engine –

– and the driver side window shattered in.

He had moved so impossibly fast there was no space to even react. His hand was through the glass, pulling up the lock, opening the door, dragging me out. Then he held me there against the car. His face was smeared with blood and two of his teeth were too long. Light flowed from his eyes.

I think I was screaming over and over, "Please let me go, please – let me go –"

He laughed and shook his head. "No way. You're my *dessert.*"

I found a last reserve of determination, then, and answered, "Fine, but before you kill me look at the album on the ground behind you."

It was where I had dropped the album. His eyes flicked around, saw the object. Then he threw me to the ground, hard, and turned to grab the album. I lay there, hurting, hoping, while he went through the pages of his book. His expression didn't change, but he began to turn each page slower, taking longer to study the photos.

To appraise his work.

Finally he closed it, dropped it back in the car. "So?"

"So I want people to know about your tags."

"People *do* know."

"But only the ones around here."

He frowned for a moment, then walked away from me to where Bad Teeth lay dead on the cracked sidewalk. He leaned down, drove his hand into the dead man's midsection, pulled it out wet and sticky. Then he went to the wall and fingerpainted, finishing his signature. Wiping his hand clean on his shirt, he told me, "Blood's no good after they're dead, so I use it for the tag."

Was he offering himself to me? I took the chance. "Let me write about you. For the newspaper. I can sell them an article, a big article. You tell me what to say, that's all I'll put in. It'll be just about you, why you do it, what you're saying – "

"So all the Beverly Hills assholes can go, like, 'Oh, now I see,' that it?"

"Yes," I answered, "and maybe then they won't be so anxious to paint over your stuff."

"Who's painting over me?" he demanded.

"Not other taggers. People who think it's graffiti, vandalism."

"And you think you can stop that?"

"You can't by yourself, Cazador," I told him. "Sure, you can take out a couple of stoned gangbangers, maybe some unarmed stupid little girl, but you can't stand up to the rest of the world alone."

After a long pause he toed the corpse of Bad Teeth. "What about him? You saw what I did."

Was there a hint of self-disgust there? I started to pull myself up. "Yes, I did."

"And?"

"Too much bad crack, Caz."

He smiled and I saw with relief that those long teeth didn't look so long any more. "Hey, you're pretty brave, y'know? Dumber 'n shit, but brave. Maybe I talk to you."

"Yes, talk to me. But you've got to guarantee my safety when we're done."

He spread his hands in mock resignation. "Now, how can *anyone* do that in this neighborhood, huh?" Then, bending close to me, he said, "You're in my world, so you're gonna take what I give, okay?"

He strode off a few feet and reached for a backpack he must have brought with him, opened it and pulled out paint cans, several of which he jammed into his cavernous baggy pants pockets. Then he went to his mural and called back to me, "I show you how I paint, but you can't write it, okay?"

I muttered agreement and asked if I could turn on my car headlights. He said no, I'd have to use my night vision. He floated up twenty feet and began to paint.

I should have been terrified, or incredulous. I should have scrambled for safety, screamed for help, gotten in my car and squealed out of there. Instead I felt only... *rightness.* It all fit together now and watching I believed it was his fervor that lifted him. In the dark I could see his arms move, first contained and precise, next in grand sweeping arcs, and colors appeared. He layered them, the colors; he had special nozzles he switched between cans; he knew his materials with the intimacy required of any great artist. Sometimes he masked areas with his hand, carelessly letting the blue or red or black whoosh out across his brown skin.

And all the time he talked. He told me about how he'd been just another Hispanic gangbanger, ditching school and chasing girls, until at thirtenn he'd discovered he could paint. At fifteen the police had caught him and he'd done six months in a juvie honor camp. While there he'd heard rumors about "some crazyass motherfucker in Echo Park" who sucked blood like Dracula and he wanted that so he could paint forever. Upon release from the honor camp he'd gone searching and on a dark, cloudy Saturday night had found what he'd been searching for – or, rather, it had found *him.* He'd managed to bite his assailant before he was drained and so he had turned. Now he disguised his feedings as gang acts, letting the press draw the conclusions for him. His family watched over him in the day, protecting their treasure, their Cazador.

"Do they know what you are?" I asked.

"I dunno. I think they gotta, but... don' ask, don' tell, kinda the way it is in my house, comprénde?"

The sky was purpling by the time he came back down to earth. Even in that shallow light I could see the finished work was magnificent. Even if I didn't remember everything he'd told me the new tag was a living document, would endure.

I squinted at the violet sky, and shivered in the morning chill. "It's almost dawn. Would you get hurt if..."

"You ever forget you left shit on the barbecue?" he asked.

I laughed, despite my cold and my hurts and the dead boy twenty feet away. "Will you make it?"

"No problem. I don't live far, an' you wouldn' believe how fuckin fast I can run now."

A car drove by a block away. Early workers, beginning to file back to the few buildings still functioning in this urban hell. "How can I reach you again?"

"You can't," he answered.

"But I – "

He interrupted, "My deal, remember? You jus' go home, write the story, get it in the paper. Not like I need the money, after all."

I nodded – then jumped at the sound of a voice behind me. "Freeze!"

I whirled to see a man fifty feet away, holding a gun out. Where... ? Then I realized – he'd been in that car that had driven past.

    – He walked closer. "I'm making a citizen's arrest."

    As he neared, revealed in the dim light, I recognized him. It took me a minute to make the connection, then it burst out of me: "Henry. Henry Colson. I saw you on the news."

    Henry smiled, but didn't waver his grip on the pistol he held steady. "That's right, you're face to face now with a local hero."

    "Right. Now put the gun away, Henry, that's –"

    "Shut up! He's the one I want." He waved the gun at El Cazador. "I heard it on my police scanner. When they took his friend to the hospital to fix his broken arm. Lucky me, I beat the cops. Guess they got other shitheads to worry about, so I'm holding you until they get here."

    I glanced at El Cazador, knowing what he must be thinking: Henry would get more than a citizen's arrest in about twenty minutes, when the sun edged up past the horizon.

    The Hunter wasn't going to wait.

    He launched himself at Henry. He was little more than a streak, a crazy panel out of a comic book. Henry panicked and popped off a shot before Caz plowed into him.

    The shot hit me.

    The impact threw me down, then the pain hit. It was in my left shoulder. There was blood everywhere – *and o god it was my blood my blood this time spilling out* –

    I heard Henry scream as something ripped. Then El Cazador was over me, his face smeared with Henry's blood, his eyes actually concerned. "Son of a bitch, man, he got you – "

I think I told him to go.

He never saw. Never saw Henry, not dead yet, his chest laid open, his mouth an "O" of astonishment and agony, the gun still in his fingers, bringing it up, firing, once, twice...

El Cazador toppled. Two holes in his chest.

I got to my knees. I looked at Henry first, to see if he would fire again. He was on his back, eyes open, staring at the cobalt blue sky. I thought he was dead.

Cazador was coughing, trying to lift his head to look at the wounds. "Shit," he muttered.

My hands fluttered above him helplessly. "I thought bullets couldn't kill you."

"They can't, but the blood's leakin' out, makin' me... making me weak. If I don't get blood... I won't make it home before... before..."

"What about Henry?"

El Cazador's nose wrinkled. "I can smell him from here – he's dead, the motherfucker. Can't have dead blood."

"Then take me."

He blinked at me in surprise. "You been shot, already lost blood. I could kill you..."

"El Cazador will die otherwise."

I put my wrist to his mouth. I was shaking, from cold, from shock, from weakness, from terror. He pulled the wrist away and I thought he was refusing me. Then he gently pushed me down and rolled towards me. There was nothing beautiful about his scarred face as it bent over me, I could smell the blood and paint on him, I could feel his weight... but when his teeth slid into my neck, what I saw was beautiful, glorious, transcendent. I saw his art, all his tags, the way he saw them. I saw the colors, the layers of shimmering shades, the figures so vivid they seemed to move if you turned your gaze to the side. I felt the rage and the pride and the desperation. It was all there before me, a magnificent panorama of vision.

A vision worth dying for.

But I didn't die.

When I came to I was in the back of an ambulance, on the way to St. Joseph's.

It turned out the police had come about the time the sun had risen. They'd found Henry Colson and the boy with bad teeth. At first they'd believed me to be a third corpse, but the paramedics found a weak pulse and started transfusions immediately.

Of course they asked me what had happened. I told them I'd been following Henry Colson for a story and he'd been attacked when he'd foolishly tried to step into a gang rumble. They didn't believe me, but it made as much sense as anything else.

I got out ten days later and wrote the first story. Of course it didn't say El Cazador could float or drank blood or would live forever as a 16-year-old kid. What it did say was good enough that the paper did publish it. They even put it in the Sunday magazine; you probably read it, then forgot it as your weekend wore on. The check helped defray part of my hospital costs. One production company called, but nothing much ever came of it. Meanwhile, a major studio has gone into production on **THE HENRY COLSON STORY.**

I'm still waitressing these days. I haven't thought much about writing again. Sometimes I do, then I see the scars, the ones in my shoulder and throat.

El Cazador disappeared, no new tags. For a while I thought he hadn't made it, that my blood had not been enough, that he'd been snuffed out by the sun's blistering whiteness, vaporized into nothingness.

Then one day I was on my shift when four Mexican kids came into the restaurant. They sat, giggling and joking among themselves. I went to pour coffee – and nearly dropped the pot.

One of them was wearing an expensive jacket with an airbrushed painting on the back, showing a brown fist hovering in the air over the Los Angeles skyline.

It was unmistakably his work.

I asked the kid where he'd gotten the jacket. Something in my face or voice must have told him I was serious, because he stopped kidding around, looked at me and said only, "What diff'rence does it make?"

I nodded and knew he was right.

Born to Wear Black

Denise Dumars

She stopped at the 7-Eleven on 120th Street after work. Get something to go with whatever she had at home to cook for dinner, go home, cook it, go to bed, get up the next day, and do it all over again. What a crazy way we all live, she thought.

"Big night at the 7-Eleven," she said aloud to herself as she pulled into the nearly-full parking lot. Wasn't much else for kids to do at this end of town – hang around the convenience store, panhandle, make prank phone calls, maybe wait until dark and graffiti a little on the side of the building. Hawthorne had never been a kid-friendly town; it had begun as a bedroom community for aerospace workers, and since the recession it was sliding rapidly toward ghettohood.

Two teenagers working up just such a prank phone call routine watched her as she got out of the Ciera and went inside. They made faces when they noticed her noticing them.

She tried to remember which aisle the salsa was stacked on while wedging her way through the line in front of the lottery ticket counter. The magazine aisle, she seemed to remember.

He was standing in front of the magazines, staring at the rack of bright covers, not moving. He's very handsome, she thought, taking in the overall view of him: longish black hair waving about the shoulders, fair skin, black polo shirt and black jeans. He was just a bit shorter than her five-seven, but was well-proportioned with long legs. She liked long legs.

He looks like somebody, she thought. Somebody on TV; now who is it? She felt her face flush as she moved past him to the part of the aisle where the Ortega salsa was advertised.

"'Scuse me," he said, startling her. "Would you have 50 cents for a soda?" He seemed to be asking it of her feet. He finally raised his head and she could see his eyes were black.

He looks a little like Alan Rickman, she thought. That's the actor he looks like. Without thinking she gave him 50 cents.

"Thank you," he said, and started to walk away. Then he stopped. "Bright blessings," he added, and went to the refrigerated case, got out a Coke, and took it to the counter.

She stood there with her mouth open. That's the first bum I've ever seen who actually did what he said he was going to do with the money he begged, she thought. He's a homeless person, she finally realized. She looked at his back, noticing now that his pants were slightly baggy and ill-fitting, and both the shirt and pants were faded. She felt a slight shudder of revulsion at the idea that she'd found herself momentarily attracted to a homeless person...especially after the strange way he acted and the strange thing he said. She felt sorry for him; he was so young. How could someone so young be so lost?

She went home and made herself some quesadillas. They almost burned while she opened her mail. Bills, a nasty letter from the hospital stating that "your insurance hasn't paid us yet," a sappy card from her mother, and magazine subscription renewal slips. She caught the quesadillas in time and ate them with the Ortega salsa while watching the news.

After dinner she took the mail into the extra bedroom that served as her "office" and put them down on the desk amidst a pile of similar stuff. She opened the drapes and watched the planes coming in to Los Angeles International Airport for a moment in the twilight.

A bit of black down by the sidewalk caught her eye. It was the young homeless man! He was down the block, standing in front of an apartment building identical to the one she lived in, but for being painted green. He was staring straight ahead with the same rapt look he'd had at the magazine rack at the 7-Eleven. It was hard for her to take her eyes off of him. She closed the drapes.

Perusing the *TV Guide*, she forgot about him. *Star Trek* (she called all versions of it by the same generic name) was a rerun – nothing else on except tabloid shows looking through celebrities' dirty underwear. It seemed there was nothing left for her to do but straighten up the place – always the last priority.

It was almost dark, but it was still hot out. She gathered up the garbage, and walked down the stairs. Once outside she admired the purple sky that was giving up the last bit of sunlight.

Then she saw him again.

He was sitting on the curb in front of the house next door. He was sitting like a little kid, holding his knees, rocking softly. He was looking perfectly natural in the growing darkness, looked born to wear black, born to blend in with the night. He also looked very alone, very tired, and very hungry.

She knew it was stupid to approach him – but hey, if he tried anything she'd scream and the people in the house next door or the other apartments would come running (she knew almost all her neighbors). He looked so small and frail, so young.

She approached him carefully. "Hello again," she said.

He smiled. Gratefully, she thought.

"Would you like something to eat?"

"Yes, if it is no trouble."

"No trouble at all. Would you like to come upstairs with me?"

He smiled again. "You are so kind," he said, and stood up.

"What's your name?"

"My name is Lew," she thought he said. His voice was very soft, and traffic was loud on the nearby boulevard.

"I'm Karen. Nice to meet you, Lew."

He followed her up the stairs to her apartment. Her back door was open, and one could easily see in through the metal security screen door which was locked. She wasn't worried once she'd gotten next to him – he seemed completely harmless, if rather flummoxed, and shy.

He walked in and stood with the same rapt stare she'd seem him exhibit before. "Sit down at the table," she directed.

He smiled again, this time looking her in the eye for the first time. "Your name should be Freya," he said suddenly. "You have green eyes like a cat."

She laughed, self-conscious. "Other people have said that I have eyes like a cat, but you're the first one who said I should be named 'Freya.'"

He sat down at the table, looking down at it, a slight smile on his placid face. I wonder if he's on some kind of medication, she thought to herself. Jeez, this is weird, I mean, bringing in some homeless guy...why am I doing this?

She fixed him quesadillas, which he ate gratefully, grimacing at the heat of the salsa, but eating it greedily nonetheless.

Then he got up from the table. "You are so kind," he said. "I will go now. Bright blessings..."

"Lew?" she said. "Would you...would you like to take a shower before you go? I can wash your clothes in the laundry room."

He seemed to consider it. "Oh. Yes, that would be wonderful. Flowing water...I miss it."

Karen went into the bathroom and took a towel from the rack. "I'll put a clean towel in the bathroom for you. Put your clothes in this and hand them to me through the door."

He disappeared into the bathroom. Soon, a slim white arm appeared around the door and handed her the bundle of clothes in the towel. She marveled at the fairness of his skin next to her olive hand as she took the bundle from him.

She thought long and hard, and then she went downstairs and threw the bundle into the washer with some detergent.

She waited until she heard him turn off the water. Then she knocked on the bathroom door. "Would you like something to drink?" she asked him.

"Yes," he answered, "What is it?"

"White grape juice," she said, handing him a glass through the barely open door.

"Good!" he said, more loudly than anything he'd said so far. She nodded to herself. She was sure now.

He did not come out of the bathroom. She waited. After a while he said, so softly again that she could barely hear him, "Are my clothes done yet?"

She pushed open the bathroom door. "Would you like to lie down and get some rest? You can stay here tonight if you like."

His black eyes opened very wide, the dark lashes standing out against his white face. He was biting his lower lip and looked very vulnerable with only the towel clutched around himself. He swallowed, hard.

She stepped toward him, and put her arms around him. His skin was cool, and as Karen hugged him she thought, he's so small, my shoulders are broader than his...

He clutched the towel desperately with one hand and with the other he embraced her.

She stepped away from him. "Let me dry your hair," she said, and ran her fingers through the silky black waves. Then she snatched the towel from him, and twirled it around his head, rubbing his hair vigorously, laughing.

He said nothing and made strange little noises in his throat. He stood and submitted to her ministrations. Then she hung the towel on the rack and took his hand. He looked at her buxom, naked body and followed her into the bedroom.

Pale and cool in the moonlight, he kissed her full lips. One of his small hands caressed her breast. His skin was beautiful. He was slim and hard all over, his bone structure exquisitely sculpted.

Trailing off into sleep sometime later, she felt happier than she had in a long time.

In the morning, she got up when the alarm went off. She showered quickly, and went back into the bedroom. She listened to his chest, his neck. No pulse, no respiration. She dressed and ran down to the laundry room to get his clothes. She handled them with the plastic gloves she'd taken out of the package of hair dye she planned to use soon.

Up in the apartment, she began to dress him, which was far more difficult than she'd expected. Suddenly she stopped.

"Shit!" she cried aloud to herself. "I wonder...goddamn DNA testing..." Just in case, she got a washcloth out of the bathroom and cleaned any traces of herself from his genitals. Then she dressed him, albeit sloppily and with great difficulty, and took him down to the garage. The street was quiet as it was on any work day. Every good, industrious, hard-working descendent of the Indo-Europeans doing what they ought to be doing.

She slid him into the back seat of her car. "If only your ancestors had stayed in the Hebrides, darling..." she said to his corpse.

She regretted being late for work, but the only place she could think of to leave him was twenty miles away. Once she got off the Long Beach Freeway, she found an alley to place him in, almost right next to a wino who stank from wetting himself in his sleep. And then she went to work.

The boss looked at her funny as she walked in late, but she stood strong and tall, proud to be an Indo-European, proud to have eliminated yet another of the Faery breed from this shore, another of the breed who should have stayed behind the stone walls her people built and in the daytime darkness of Lapland. Merry meet and merry part, and merry meet again, she thought to herself, thinking of poor dead Lew; he was he prettiest one of his breed she'd ever met.

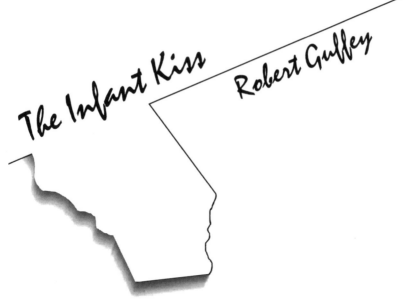

The Infant Kiss

Robert Guffey

The words hit her like a stone against the head.

"I'm afraid the cancer has metastasized. Damn it, Jennifer, why didn't you come to see me sooner?"

Andrew sat down in his vinyl swivel chair, his weak posture indicating a completely broken spirit. He placed his forehead in his hands. Jennifer thought he looked even more depressed by the news than she did.

For a few moments she didn't say anything. She glanced around Andrew's office, staring blankly at the colorless decor. It was as dull as Andrew himself. Their house would've been just as sterile if she hadn't immediately rolled up her sleeves and attacked it and poured life into it. She'd seen their house – Andrew's house now – since her departure. The life had leaked out of it once again, as if Andrew alone was enough to suck the color from his surroundings. She didn't know how she'd managed to stay married to him for six whole years before she'd finally cut out on him. They were so incompatible. Even more mysterious was the fact that he still seemed to be in love with her.

Now he'll blame the cancer on the divorce, she thought. Anything to get me back.

Finally, with a loss for anything truly meaningful to say, Jennifer whispered, "I – I thought it was a mole."

Andrew closed his eyes. He seemed to be holding tears back. "We'll have to do surgery, cut it off and hope it doesn't come back. If it does, maybe radiation – "

"Andrew, I was married to you for six years. For *six years* I heard you complain about all the patients who died right after radiation or the hundreds of failed attempts at surgery. You think I'm going to let you put me through that?"

He just looked at her, blinking as if through a fog. "What other choice is there? Are you just going to let yourself die?"

Without meeting his accusatory gaze she said, "I don't know. I'll have to think about it." She rose from the chair.

"Wait a second," Andrew said, a rising panic in his voice. The metal legs of the chair scraped against the hard, antiseptic floor; it created a noise like cat claws scraping against a chalkboard. He stood in front of her, blocking her path out the door. "You can't leave yet. Look, you're not going to be able to handle a situation like this on your own. Why don't you move back into the house? I can take care of you. I'll make sure you get the best care – " He reached out, lovingly placed his hands on her shoulders. There was a hint of desperation in his touch.

Jennifer twisted out of his grasp. "You never change,

you never *listen.* I left you because you wouldn't let me handle anything on my own. Now that I *am* handling my own life you think I'm just going to turn it over to you again?"

"Jennifer, you're *dying* – "

"It's hopeless anyway, is that it? So I should just put it in your hands? If anyone's going to kill me it might as well be you?"

" You *know* that's not what I mean." His voice rose in anger for a moment. In mid-sentence, however, it trailed off into a whisper. Apparently he didn't want the other patients outside to hear.

Jennifer placed her hand on the doorknob. "Look, I just want to get a second opinion, okay? It's as simple as that." She just wanted to get out of that claustrophobic office.

Andrew began to reach out for her again, then abruptly drew his hands back. A baby reaching for fire. "I – I love you."

Jennifer kept her eyes focused on the floor. "I'd like to get a second opinion on that too," she said, then left the office without once looking back.

It had been a mistake to go see him, Jennifer thought as she took the bus to work. For once she'd let her pocketbook get in the way of her pride. She hadn't had enough money to go to any other doctor. She'd known he would give her a checkup for free. Presumably two years would've been enough time for both of them to simply regard their relationship as a thing of the past. But Andrew just couldn't let go.

For a second the idea passed through her mind that Andrew had *lied* about the cancer simply to convince her to move back in with him. No. Now that was real paranoia, she thought. She didn't believe he was capable of such a thing. He didn't have the imagination for it.

Finally the bus stopped just outside Mrs. Hempnill's Handy Market, where she'd been working for the past few months. A billowing, gray cloud of smoke blew into her face as the bus pulled away from the curb. She coughed, wondering why her cancer surprised her. Everyone living in Los Angeles should have had it by now. Perhaps they did.

For a second she just stared up at the vaulting blueness of the sky. So much death there.

As usual, Jennifer began work at one o'clock in the afternoon. The small grocery market could only afford to hire someone part-time, even though they actually needed a full-time employee. Jennifer was happy to take the part-time position. There were no other jobs available anywhere else. Besides, the market was only a few blocks away from where she rented a dismal little room in a dismal little building. The one-room cubicle, which she shared with a hundred or so roaches, was the only place she could afford to live.

At the moment Jennifer was trying to ring through the cash register a great many items as fast as she could. A line was forming behind the small Asian woman Jennifer was presently dealing with. She hated it when there was a long line of people all staring at her, waiting for her to serve them. Combined with the damn cramps she'd been having all morning, the tension was almost enough to push her over the edge completely. It was days like these that she hated being a woman.

The Asian lady had only one more item – a pound of cherries – left to ring up. *Thank God,* Jennifer thought as she reflexively punched in $1.20 for the cherries. She proceeded to bag the groceries. "That'll be $40.48 all together, please," said Jennifer.

The Asian woman shook her head back and forth. She pulled out a pen and a notepad and began scribbling furiously.

"Tell me your name," she said.

"Excuse me?"

"Your name, please. You're being fined."

"What're you talking about?" The customers behind the woman were growing restless.

The woman sighed and flashed an official-looking identification card. "I'm Gina Yamamoto from the Department of Weights and Measures. The legal price for a pound of cherries is ninety-nine cents. You overcharged me a total of *twenty-two* cents. You're to be fined $550. Sign here."

She ripped a sheet of paper from the notepad and pointed at a blank space near the bottom. Jennifer snatched it from her and merely stared at it. "I didn't overcharge you," she said. "A pound of cherries has always been a dollar twenty."

The owner of the market, a pudgy woman named Mrs. Hempnill who looked like a kind old grandmother from a Norman Rockwell painting, appeared on the scene long enough to say, "Oh no, dear. We changed the rules this afternoon. Don't you remember?" She said this with a nervous tremor in her voice.

"You never told me anything!" Mrs. Hempnill quickly shuffled away, claiming she had to go wait on a customer.

"You must sign your name," Ms. Yamamoto repeated, shoving a silver pen into Jennifer's fist. Angrily, Jennifer signed the paper and threw it back into Yamamoto's prunish face. She perused the signature, then gasped. "You can't sign 'Richard Nixon'! This is a legal document! That'll be another $275." She scribbled some more.

"This is crazy. Let's say I did overcharge you; it's only twenty-two *cents*!"

"So you admit to overcharging me!" said Yamamoto, withdrawing a small notepad from her purse. "You're going to be sorry when you have to appear before a judge if you don't sign your name to this sheet."

"A judge?! Look, I'm not signing anything. I did nothing wrong."

"Very well, then." She jotted something down in the notebook. "Refuses to sign her name," she mumbled to herself, then stuffed the notebook back into her purse. She gave Jennifer yet another slip of paper. "You'll be receiving your court date in the mail." Ms. Yamamoto strode out of the market on stiff, stubby legs.

Though the customers were now loudly demanding to be waited on, Jennifer abandoned her cash register and found Mrs. Hempnill near the meat section pricing packs of ribs. "What the hell was that all about?" Jennifer asked. She showed Hempnill the slip of paper, on which was printed the amount of the fine. "I can't afford to pay this."

"Well, neither can I dear," she replied, smiling pleasantly. "Besides, it wasn't my fault. I warned you."

"You never said a damn thing!"

"You *must* not have heard me." Hempnill's smile had disappeared. "You have customers to be waited on."

Jennifer realized that she could not afford to lose this job, even with a $550 fine hanging above her head. She couldn't argue with the owner or else she'd get booted out of the market quicker than she'd left Andrew. Even with a weekly paycheck she couldn't keep up the payments on her single room. If only the roaches would volunteer to chip in their fair share; but that would never happen. She had to make do with the situation as it now existed. That entailed keeping her job no matter what.

She nodded at the owner and said, "Sorry for disturbing you. I'll leave you to your work." The owner turned her back on Jennifer, who sped over to the angry mob of customers milling around her cash register. As she began ringing up items, she wondered if she was going to get hit by another government fine. Maybe this time the FDA would hit her up for a $1000 because she overcharged a cent on a single gumball. Anything seemed possible now.

During the bus ride home later that afternoon, the amount of the fine twirled about ominously in her head: $550... $550... $550... Not to mention the extra $275 for refusing to sign the form. All because some little bureaucratic martinet had a stick up her ass and needed to take it out on someone less powerful than her. Jennifer felt as if she were being strong-armed into paying protection money to the Mafia. ("*If you don't cough up the cash, sister, you lose your job. Period.*") The Mafia, the Department of Weights and Measures—what the hell was the difference between them? At least in the Mafia you were rewarded for working hard. In the "above ground" job market you worked and worked and worked, and your only payment was being able to keep your job.

Sitting beside her on the bus was a discarded copy of the *L.A. Spotlight*. Idly, she glanced at the Classifieds. In between two ads (one marked "Bisexual White Female, Into Vampires, Seeks Type-0 Negative Black Transvestite" and the other "Single White Male Seeks A Quiet Housewife-Type Who Doesn't Mind A Little Bestiality From Time To Time") she found the following:

Nonconformists Unite!
Are You Tired
Of Meaningless Rules & Expectations
You Can Never Live Up To?
Are Rules Making You *Sick Inside?*
Are They *Killing You Slowly?!*
Cheer Up!
The Answer Is Before Your Eyes!
Call (310) 451-1224!
Or Come See Us At 512 Santa Monica Blvd.

There was definitely something wrong with this world. Of course, she had known that for a long time, but her experience with Ms. Yamamoto had served to fortify this conviction. The problem was this: rules. There were so many rules in the world that civilization was being strangled by noose-shaped red tape. This gradual constriction was cutting off the circulation of blood to everyone's brain. It was making everyone silly and stupid. It was making everyone obedient to nonsensical *rules*. What was needed was an abolishment of rules — *all rules*.

She glanced back at the ad. 512 Santa Monica Boulevard wasn't far from the Nuart Theater, where Jennifer had seen a midnight showing of *Eyes Without A Face* only a few weeks before. She was very familiar with the area, and yet she couldn't quite remember what building occupied that address.

She was curious now. Though she probably wouldn't go inside, she simply wanted to see what the place would look like. Probably seedy as hell. Like her apartment.

She didn't feel like conversing with the cockroaches in her living room at the moment, so...

In between a coffee shop and a New Age bookstore stood a building marked 512. It appeared to be abandoned. Boards were nailed over the empty windows, and yet hanging on the doorknob was a sign that read OPEN. She tried to turn the knob, but it wouldn't budge.

"The entrance is in the back," said a high-pitched voice.

She looked around, but couldn't see anybody.

"Down here."

A boy peered up at her through an open basement window. He was about nine years old. He had dark hair and eyes to match – eyes that immediately ducked out of view once she kneeled down to speak to him. The window slammed shut.

Curious now, Jennifer circled the building and found a second door in the alley. The door was wide open. She entered a large room filled with nothing but packing crates stacked on top of each other. They nearly touched the ceiling. The only other object in the room was a mahogany desk, behind which sat the little boy. He was busy writing in a spiral notebook.

"Excuse me," she said.

The boy looked up at her. He possessed an open, innocent, penetrating gaze that seemed to strip away the tenuous layers of calm she'd constructed around the grief lodged deep inside her. He moved his lips, but no sound emerged. He ripped a page out of the notebook and handed it to Jennifer. In large, flowery writing the message read: I Love You.

"Oh, how sweet," Jennifer said.

The boy ripped out another page and handed it to her. This one read: I Want To Fuck You.

"Hey, now wait a minute," she said.

The boy smiled and darted through a doorway behind him. For a second Jennifer considered running in the opposite direction, but her curiosity nagged at her to at least peek through the doorway and see what lay beyond.

The adjoining room was, in fact, a movie set. A camera crew encircled a mock living room. Strangely, the set resembled her own apartment. On the couch – her own couch – lay a man and a woman. Both were naked. The woman reared up on all fours while the man thrust his penis into her asshole. Jennifer instantly recognized the woman as Gina Yamamoto, the inspector who had given her the fine. Stranger still, the man was her ex-husband Andrew. As Yamamoto yowled like a cat in heat, Andrew turned and flashed Jennifer a wide smile. He said, "How you doing, honey?" On the carpet right in front of the couch lay Andrew's receptionist Sylvia, who was performing cunnilingus on old Mrs. Hempnill. Hempnill's meaty hands clutched Sylvia's long blonde hair, pushed her face deeper into her flabby thighs. Sylvia seemed all too eager to obey.

Manning the cameras were dozens and dozens of the little boys. Each was identical to the other.

"Would you like to join in?" Andrew asked.

"What – what the hell is this?" Jennifer said.

"Just trying to break some rules, that's all. Isn't that what you wanted?"

She backed away toward the door. She whispered, "I just wanted to be well again."

"Then you better join in. It feels good to let go, trust me. I *am* a doctor, after all.'

Mrs. Hempnill cackled at that line.

The bus driver who'd dropped Jennifer off on Santa Monica Boulevard suddenly emerged from behind the couch, as naked as the others. This was an obese black man in his late fifties. Without interrupting Sylvia and Hempnill, he spread Sylvia's ass cheeks and entered her from behind. "Listen to the doctor," said the bus driver as he thrust back and forth, "he sure knows what he's talkin' about. Boy, this shit's fun as hell!"

One of the cameras swiveled around to film her re-action. She found herself staring at her distorted re-flection in the curved surface of the lens.

Andrew said, "You're never going to beat this sick-ness if you hold onto your old way of thinking. That's what got you to this point in the first place."

The bus driver said, "Hey, sweetie, if you're not going to join in, could you run and get me some Vaseline? This chick's as tight as a miser's wallet."

Jennifer ran out of the room, past the towers of crates, and into the dingy alley. She didn't remember much after that.

An hour or so later she entered her second-floor apartment, half-expecting to see the movie set once more. Though the set had been an exact duplicate of her living room, there were no "actors" lounging on the floor and the couch. The room was empty.

As usual she locked the door behind her immediately upon entering the room. She poured herself a small glass of red wine, hoping it would ease the tension in her neck and shoulder. She sighed as she sat down on the couch and stared at the gray TV screen. Something prevented her from turning it on.

She'd taken four or five sips from her wine before finally noticing the white piece of paper that sat on the glass coffee table in front of her. It was neatly folded in two. Half of it was sticking up in the air; a breeze from an open window caused it to bob up and down ever so slightly. Somehow, Jennifer knew it didn't belong to her.

As she leaned forward to pick it up, she saw the boy sitting at the opposite end of the couch. He was about nine years old.

He had dark hair and eyes to match – an open, innocent, penetrating gaze that seemed to srip away the tenuous layers of calm she'd constructed around the grief lodged deep inside her. He moved his lips, but no sound emerged.

Moments later, the boy simply . . . vanished.

Jennifer dropped the glass of wine and leaped up from the couch. A red stain spread across the beige carpet.

Jennifer just stood there for a moment, staring at nothing. An eerie feeling had coiled around her spine. She glanced from side to side, as if expecting the boy to reappear from nowhere and say, "Boo." She checked every nook and cranny in the place, found nothing. She was alone.

At last she remembered the note. She returned to the coffee table and picked up the piece of paper. She unfolded it and found four words printed sloppily in black ink: KISS ME, KILL ME.

She closed her eyes and recalled the boy's silent, moving lips. Is *that* what he had been saying?

She now felt uncomfortable in the tiny apartment. She didn't want to be alone. But the only close friend she really had in the city was Andrew, though it was hard to call him a "friend." Nevertheless she grabbed her purse and walked to a phone booth down the block. It stood outside a 7-Eleven. She dropped a few coins into the slot and dialed Andrew's office number, then stared at the numbers as they appeared on a digital readout just below the phone cradle. She asked Sylvia, the receptionist, to tell him who was on the phone. A few minutes later Andrew said, "Jennifer? I was going to go after you when you ran out of my office."

Jennifer opened her mouth to tell him about the visions, but choked on the words. Why should she tell him anything? What was he going to do about it, come over and hold her hand? Christ, the reason she'd left him was to take care of herself. Now that she was outside, among a street full of people, her fear had lessened considerably.

"Jennifer? Hello? Are you still there?"

"Yes, of course. Andrew, is it possible to see things when you're dying of cancer?"

"See things? Like what?"

"Well, like hallucinations or – "

A voice cut into the line. A young boy. Faint, hollow. Taunting:

"Jennifer . . . kiss me, kill me."

Andrew: "Jennifer? Hello? What's wrong?"

"You don't hear that?"

"Hear what?"

The boy: "Oh, Jennifer, where is thy sting? Dying is an art – "

Jennifer slammed the phone into the cradle and backed away against the glass door. Her gaze alighted upon the digital readout. Instead of numbers, words appeared: DYING IS AN ART, LIKE EVERYTHING ELSE. I DO IT EXCEPTIONALLY WELL. I DO IT SO IT FEELS LIKE HELL. THANK YOU FOR USING AT&T.

Again she glanced around as if expecting to see the Devil himself lurking outside the phone booth. She saw no such thing. She merely saw the usual pedestrians of Los Angeles: tanned old ladies walking French poodles, pale teenage girls dressed in nothing but black even beneath a hot summer sun, joggers with Walkmans clipped to their sweat-stained shorts, men in business suits on their way back to the office, beggars asking for enough change to get back home – every day, every year, the same lost people asking for just one more quarter in order to find their way home. No devils, not that she could see.

Nevertheless she felt pretty freaked-out. She slipped out of the phone booth and walked down the sidewalk at a very fast pace. She didn't want to go back to her apartment. She didn't want to run to Andrew.

A couple of blocks later she decided to stop at a small café. She sat down at a table near the window. She watched the people strolling by and thought about what she should do – about the hallucinations, about her cancer, about the fine, about her rent, about the rest of her short life. A waiter, a slim blonde kid in his late teens, approached the table and asked her what she would like.

I want my life back, she wanted to say, but suppressed the urge.

"Iced coffee," she whispered.

The kid nodded, said he'd be right back, and walked away with a jaunty bounce in his step. The kid has a nice ass, she thought. He was in his early twenties, about ten years younger than her. She couldn't believe she thought of him as a "kid." It hadn't been so long ago when she'd been working her way through college at a similar job. Her plan had been to blaze a trail through the newspaper world, be a female Bob Woodward *and*_Carl Bernstein all rolled into one, maybe topple a President or two, who knows? Anything had seemed possible back then.

It didn't quite happen that way, though. She interned at a local magazine, worked her way up to a $100-a-week paycheck, met Andrew at a party, dropped out of school, then relinquished her life to his for a whole six years. Until she'd regained her senses. A year before she'd thanked God that there had been no children to worry about amidst the fallout of their separation. Now she regretted the fact that she would never experience what it was like to give birth.

Regrets. How many can you have in one life? She was certainly going to find out before it was all over.

Somebody knocked on the window beside her, jerking her out of her reverie. The boy. He pressed a small card against the window:

DEATH IS HERE AND DEATH IS THERE,
DEATH IS BUSY EVERYWHERE

Jennifer couldn't speak. She couldn't move. The handwriting on the card was identical to that found in her apartment.

A fist knocked gently on the table top. She turned to see the boy standing beside her. He looked somewhat different up close. His torn clothes seemed to suggest he'd been living on the streets for years. He handed her a small rectangular card. She glanced downwards, expecting to find another message about death. Instead she saw a bright yellow happy face hovering over the following words:

> Please pardon my intrusion, but I am
> a DEAF-MUTE trying to earn a decent liv-
> ing. Would you help me by buying one of
> these cards. *Pay Whatever You Wish...*
> THANK YOU AND MAY
> GOD BLESS YOU ALL.

The young waiter rushed over to Jennifer's table and grabbed the boy by the elbow.

"Hey, the manager doesn't want any panhandlers in here!" He jerked his thumb over his shoulder, motioning for the boy to leave.

Jennifer glanced out the window once more. Of course, no boy stood there any longer. Slowly, as if rising from a daze, she returned her attention to the little drama unfolding before her. She stared at the bedraggled child being led out like a dog, and realized how many times she'd ignored people just like him. Somehow she knew she needed to speak to him.

"Please," she said to the waiter. "Don't make him leave. He's with me."

"What?" said the waiter.

"I said he's with me. Sit here." She uttered these last two words very deliberately, so the boy could read her lips. She pointed at the seat across from her.

The boy smiled and slid into the booth.

"Would you like some hot chocolate?" she said, just as slowly as before.

The boy didn't respond. He didn't even nod or shake his head. Jennifer turned to the waiter and smiled. "A cup of hot chocolate for my friend, please."

The waiter, somewhat confused, wrote down the order and staggered away. Some of the surrounding lookie-loos returned to their own coffee and conversation.

The boy, still smiling, handed the card to Jennifer once again. He wiggled his finger, motioning for her to turn it over. She did so. She saw spidery handwriting, black ink.

ALL AROUND, WITHIN, BENEATH,
ABOVE IS DEATH – AND WE ARE DEATH

Jennifer's gaze locked onto the boy's face. As if in slow motion, his lips began to move. The sound that emerged from them seemed to be coming from somewhere else – directly next to her ear. His voice wasn't quite in synch with his lips, like an actor in a badly dubbed foreign film.

"Jennifer, have you ever heard of a tulpa?"

"H-how do you know my name?"

"A tulpa is a thought-form, the physical manifestation of energies given off by the mind. Most people would say that tulpas don't exist. They'd be right, of course. Tulpas *don't* exist, at least not in the way normal people do."

"And how do 'normal' people exist?"

"Tentatively. Intensely."

"It sounds like the way I used to drop acid: rarely and in high doses. Be upfront, am I having one of those flashbacks my parents warned me about when I was a kid?"

The young waiter placed a cup of hot chocolate in front of the boy. He allowed the steam to waft into his nostrils, savoring the smell, before at last taking a very slow sip. As the waiter gave Jennifer her cup of iced coffee the boy said, "Please, Jennifer, there's no need to insult me. I assure you I'm not an hallucination. Hallucinations are far lesser beings than tulpas. Hallucinations only exist *inside* one's head. Tulpas exist both inside and outside."

"And you're a tulpa?"

"Of course."

"Well, uh . . . I didn't mean to offend you."

"Don't worry about it. Sometimes even tulpas themselves don't know if they're hallucinations or not. Such confusion is common."

The waiter glanced at Jennifer strangely, then walked toward another table to greet a new pair of customers.

Jennifer lowered her voice. "So why have you been hounding me?"

"I haven't been hounding you. You've been hounding yourself."

"Excuse me?"

"I'm *your* tulpa." He pointed at her head. "I came out of that pretty little skull of yours. Oh, by the way, thanks for the drink. I would've preferred some tequila, but I suppose this will do."

"Don't mention it. So why would I want to hound

myself?"

"To show you the obvious. To show you what you've been hiding from yourself."

"Which is?"

"I can't tell you outright. That's part of the rules." He emphasized that last word with a smirk. He sipped his hot chocolate, smacked his lips together. "It has to do with the truth about your cancer."

"I'll be half-dead from chemo by the time you tell me the truth about anything."

"I'm afraid your tumor isn't an hallucination."

"Wow, front-page news. This is the big surprise?"

"Nor is it *real*. At least not in the way 'normal' tumors are real." He snapped his fingers at the waiter and pointed into his cup.

Jennifer whispered, "What are you implying?"

"What do you think?"

"I don't know. That the tumor is . . . is a tulpa?"

The boy nodded. The waiter, on his way toward another table, set a fresh cup of hot chocolate in front of him without even slowing down.

"Are you saying I brought this on myself?"

The boy shook his head as he stirred the hot chocolate with a spoon. "No, not you."

"Who did then?!" She'd raised her voice. The other customers were staring at her again. She lowered her head, focused on the coffee. She could just barely see her reflection in the ice cubes at the bottom of the empty cup.

For a second the idea passed through her mind that Andrew had lied about the cancer simply to convince her to move back in with him. No. Now that was real paranoia, she thought. She didn't believe he was capable of such a thing.

He didn't have the imagination for it.

She looked into the boy's eyes, whispered, "Andrew? Is it Andrew's tulpa?"

He nodded.

"I can't believe this. Does he hate me that much?"

"No, he *loves* you that much."

Jennifer remained silent for a moment. "So what was the purpose of that weird scene with the movie set?"

"We had to . . . catch your attention." The boy grinned.

"Is that so? Well, you did a hell of a job." She sighed. "I don't understand. What am I supposed to do, waltz on over to Andrew's office and ask him to please stop killing me?"

"What good would that do? He doesn't even know he's doing this to you."

"So am I supposed to move back in with him, is that it?"

He shook his head. "Then you'd be right back where you started. The reason he can affect you to this extent is because you're still connected to him in ways you may not even be aware of. You're still dependent on him."

"How can you say that? I pay for my own groceries, my own apartment, my own coffee—not to mention your damn hot chocolate. How the hell am I still dependent on him?"

"You're dependent on the fact that you're *no longer* dependent on him. You're still proving yourself to him, even though you have nothing to prove. Absence is presence at this point in your life. You must find a way to sever the link completely. Only at that time will the tulpas who are sucking the life from you finally lose hold and disappear." The boy tipped his head back and drained the cup of its last drop of hot chocolate. He rose from the seat. He began to move away from the table, then turned back and said, "Despite appearances, I pay my own way." He flicked six coins onto the table top, then walked quickly out of the café.

She stared at the coins: three quarters, one nickel, two pennies.

Thirty-three cents short.

She lay in her bed, in the darkness, thinking about everything and nothing. Though it was half past midnight, she couldn't go to sleep. It was a hot July evening. A warm wind from the Santa Ana mountains blew through an open window and caressed her face. She closed her eyes, tried to will herself to sleep, but could think only of the day's strange events.

After the discussion in the café she'd gone to see a movie. *Any* movie, she didn't care which. She wandered into a sequel of a popular comedy from a year before; she barely recognized the stars. She sat glaring at the film through stoic, foggy eyes. Sometimes she remembered to laugh, but only when the guffaws from the rest of the moviegoers reminded her to do so.

Afterwards she didn't feel like going home so she snuck into another film playing in the room next door, something she hadn't done since high school. This second film was a thriller about a young woman being pursued by a psychotic ex-boyfriend. It didn't make her feel very good.

She finally returned home after the second movie, climbed into bed. Drank a fresh glass of wine, stripped down to a thin T-shirt and panties, kicked the covers off the mattress as the temperature quickly began to rise, tried to wish the heat away along with her damn cancerous tumor. She also wished for a round-the-world trip and a red Ferrari. Why not ask for *three* impossible things before breakfast. Hell, why not ten?

As she scrolled down the Christmas list in her mind, between items six and eight, she wished away the invisible chains tying her to work, money, sickness, a man she no longer loved, rules, *all* rules. Before she could reach item ten, Jennifer drifted off to sleep.

She awoke to someone touching her stomach.

Her eyes snapped open and she gasped, jerking away from the tiny hand. Two dark eyes stared at her from the middle of the bed.

"Please help me," said the boy. "I don't want to die."

As her heart slowly ceased racing, Jennifer propped herself up on her elbows. "Wh-why do you think you're going to die?"

"The cancer," the boy whispered and wrapped his arms around her waist. "The cancer inside me."

Jennifer patted the boy's dark hair. "The cancer's not inside you. It's inside me."

"It's inside both of us." The boy slid his hand beneath Jennifer's T-shirt. His fingers circled the aureole of her left nipple.

Jennifer held her breath for a moment. "Wh-what're you doing?" she whispered.

"Saving you. Saving both of us." The child removed his hand from her breast, kissed her stomach, her hips, rose higher.

"What are you . . . ?" She felt queasy; butterflies

brushed against the inside of her stomach.

The child didn't answer. He carefully pushed her shirt above her breasts. The tip of his tongue just barely touched the tip of her nipple, circled it slowly. She allowed her hands to rest against the back of his head. Oh, his hair was so soft.

She closed her eyes.

She saw her life as it might have been. Working her way up through the ranks of the local magazine, distinguishing herself as a creative reporter willing to write about the underbelly of the city. Willing to take notice of all the invisible people, the unfortunate majority who fall through the cracks and end up buried in the shadow of the prosperous. At twenty-four she writes a stunning article about the life of the L.A. homeless. This article brings her to the attention of the majors, draws her into the spotlight. Offers pour in –

The boy's lips graze her shoulder blades, her throat. His teeth lightly bite on her neck. Jennifer runs her hands behind his bare back, his slim delicate shoulders. Their mouths brush against each other, their tongues find each other.

– from the *L.A. Times*, the *Washington Post*, *Newsweek*, National Public Radio, and a dozen others. Rumors start spreading that she might be nominated for a Pulitzer Prize. She's on her way up. Her dreams are being fulfilled. She hopes nothing –

Jennifer's T-shirt sticks to her damp skin as she peels the shirt off and throws it onto the carpet. The child's clothes have somehow disappeared, as if they had never been there at all. She bends over him, kisses his smooth chest. She reaches between his legs. The child moans, runs his fingers through her long black hair. He whispers. "You're a corpse, Jennifer. A murderer and a victim."

She lifts her head up from his stomach. He removes his hands from her hair. She looks directly into his eyes. "What do you mean?"

He shrugs. "For since by man came death, by man came also the resurrection of the dead." He gently removes her hand from his erect penis. He shifts his body downwards, lowers his head between her legs.

Jennifer buries her face in the sweat-stained pillow. She places her hands on the back of his head. Andrew never liked to do this. He could never move his tongue the way she wanted him to. He was cold and rigid in bed. She's happy, oh so happy that she threw him out of her life. She hopes nothing –

– will prevent her from reaching the top of her field. She wants to change the world, to leave her mark. She doesn't want to end up like her father, an alcoholic, dead in an unmarked grave, or her mother, berated into submission, beaten into a hollow mannequin devoid of personality. She needs –

– ends this moment, this one perfect moment in a broken life. She's whispering something, she doesn't know what. She can't hear her own voice anymore. She can't hear anything except the sound of rushing air inside her ears, a muffled sound like the inside of a sea shell. It's as if all her senses have been rerouted through her skin; the sights, the sounds, the smells have all become tactile. She feels like a raw nerve, an open wound bared for sensation, whether it's pleasure or pain doesn't matter any longer. The young boy removes his bloody tongue from deep inside her and crawls up her body like a pale spider. She places her hands on his tiny buttock and guides him inside. She cocks her head back, opens her mouth. A single tear trickles down her cheek. The boy buries his face into her hair, which blankets the pillow like a river. The boy whispers something into her ear. What is it? She can just barely hear the words, as if they're being spoken through a defective phone many miles away: *Death is here and death is there. Death is busy everywhere. All around, within, beneath. Above is death, and we are –*

– some recognition, just a little validation that she actually exists before her life becomes forfeit and Jennifer is reclaimed by –

– death. "We are death," she repeats, suddenly realizing that this is the very phrase she's been whispering for the past ten, twenty, thirty minutes. Perhaps longer. Perhaps forever. As long as this strange sweet sensation can last, this open red wound kiss, this ocean blood sea shell kiss, this perfect infant kiss.

She awoke in darkness. Her white sheets were stained with blood. As a child she remembered asking her mother how anyone could bleed for five days and not die. Her mother couldn't say. "That's just the way it is," she'd explained impatiently. Twenty years later Jennifer wrapped the sheets around her waist and stood in the middle of the room, searching for any trace of her nocturnal visitor. Had it all been a dream?

No. She knew very well that she never dreamed.

Crimson digital numbers glowed brightly in the darkness: 4:51. The sun would be up soon. Even though she could only have gotten a few hours sleep, she felt wide awake. A cool breeze was blowing through the window. It smelled of salt, the nearby Pacific. The scorching Santa Ana winds must have blown towards the north.

She stood there for a moment, allowing the breeze to tickle the back of her neck. She decided she would take a shower, then go for a walk — to the doctor's office. Andrew, the consummate workaholic, had been keeping his office open six days a week ever since their separation. He opened at eight a.m. on Saturdays. She simply wanted to apologize for hanging up on him the previous afternoon, and to tell him that she wouldn't be seeing him any longer. Not for medical treatment, not for anything.

The breeze felt like tiny fingers running through her long hair.

The door marked DR. ANDREW TULLY was already halfway open. Jennifer pushed it aside to find an empty waiting room. Not since the day it had first opened for business had she seen the waiting room empty. Where were all the patients? It was almost nine o'clock. It should've been full by now.

She approached the receptionist's desk, but it too was empty. Where was Sylvia? She'd been working in Andrew's office for years. At one time Jennifer had hoped that Sylvia would take poor old Andrew off her hands, but no. Sylvia was engaged to someone else.

Though she felt uncomfortable doing it, Jennifer barged into the examination room where she found Sylvia standing in the middle of the room. She had her arms crossed over her chest; she seemed to be staring at an open window.

"Sylvia?" she said.

Sylvia spun around. "Oh, Mrs. Tully, you startled

me." She still called Jennifer Mrs. Tully. It was vaguely annoying. "You don't know where Andrew is, do you?" Her voice was laced with panic.

"No. Isn't he here?"

"I-I don't know!" Sylvia wrung her hands. "The last time I saw him was around 7:30, *right here.*" She pointed at the spot where she now stood. "I went into the waiting room to talk to a patient for a couple of minutes, then came back here and found . . . well, nothing. He was gone! I'm telling you, Mrs. Tully, there's no way out of this room."

"He just . . . vanished?"

"At first I thought he might've... well, gone out the window. What with his problems with you and all, I mean. But there's no trace of him. I checked!"

Jennifer walked toward the window and stuck her head out. She looked at the sidewalk far below, at all the busy pedestrians streaming back and forth, back and forth. How many of them were human beings, and how many tulpas?

Sylvia continued talking. "I was so scared I sent all the patients home. I don't know whether I should call the police or not. What do you think?"

Jennifer glanced up at the sky. It was so clear today, so blue. She could even see the distant mountains from here. The hot winds had blown the smog north, at least for a little while. The ocean breeze that had arrived during the night now whispered in her ear: *You've been hounding yourself. You're connected to Andrew in ways you may not even be aware of.*

"They won't find him," Jennifer said quietly. *Kiss me, kill me.*

"Mrs. Tully?" Sylvia's voice was filled with confu-

sion.
    On the street below, the pedestrians   slow   ly
dis   ap   peared   one
                          by
                                                 one

Driving the Last Spike
Brian Hodge

The last time he'll see her, Kerry will still be young, about the same as she is now. The last time he'll see her, she will be reaching for his hand. The last time he'll see her, there won't be any tears – tears are for situations where there's still the hope of turnaround.

Her hair will still be blond, but the roots will be growing out, auburn, nothing to have been ashamed of in the first place. The cut won't have changed, falling close to her shoulders with her bangs trimmed straight across her brows, west coast Cleopatra with eyes blinking from out of an ash-gray blur, painted onto her face or across the horizon. Their Pacific Egypt burning, don't rule out the possibility of the sand itself baking to brittle glass in a tsunami of fire.

Or maybe it's only sunset through smog.

Garrett can't say how he knows this will be the last time he'll see her, he just does, and he doesn't need any billboard or neon sign or voices whispering in his ear.

Just because you're paranoid, we've all heard before, doesn't mean they're not out to get you.

And just because you're epileptic doesn't mean you
can't actually see the future.

*"I don't want to get into everything on the phone. You'll
understand when you get here," she told him. Only this morning? Only. Harsh 8:00 a.m. jangle the culmination of Kerry's
few days' worth of disappearance and fretting himself sick.
Sicker. "Take whatever of mine that has any value, and sell
it. Then bring me the cash. Would you do that for me?"*

"Where are you now?"

"You mean you really haven't guessed?"

"It wouldn't be Skip Ackerman's house, would it?"

She doesn't answer, and, well, that says it all, doesn't it?

The box in his arms is lighter than it looks, bulky if
little more than clothing inside, and maybe it makes
him look seedy and pathetic along the blocks of
shopfronts on Ventura Boulevard in Studio City, not
his fault there are no parking places any closer. Today's
forecast, sunny, but you knew that already. It's September and miserable, the Santa Ana wind searing
down from the mountains, full of grit and recrimina-
tion.

Ever since moving here, he has always thought of
Southern California – Los Angeles especially, a natural epicenter – as a place where great epochs go to die.
They arrive on powerful legs but are sore and rotten
inside, heaving out lungfuls of corrupted air as they
snort and bellow in fury over their lack of future.

Garrett still remembering a time, if just barely,

when he had one himself.

He's in the middle of the block when the warning flag starts to wave in his temporal lobe. Or wherever it hides in his skull – idiopathic, he has his condition but no evident cause, just born that way. Special, blessed. Once upon a more colorful time, didn't we regard epilepsy as a divine illness, God poking his vast head between those misfiring synapses and chewing on neurons?

Threw away his meds years ago after realizing that he was saner when he allowed himself to go ahead and have the seizures. Phenytoin, carbamazepine, valproic acid – into the trash with them, while he opened arms wide to his petit mal malfunction and began to love it back: You Sybil, you Delphic oracle, you polished obsidian mirror vulcanized from my own nervous system. A different story, maybe, if he was prone to swallowing his tongue, but for Garrett it's just like virtual reality, only wireless.

His stomach knows first, abruptly weightless and frustrated, wanting to fly. A flash of light that is no color in the visible spectrum, and a sense of unstable ground; the snap of gulls' wings in his ears and a smell like wet limestone in his nose. Long ago they told him his eyelids flicker and his lower jaw jerks. From onset to incapacitation takes about a minute, the reason he avoids driving in heavy traffic but has otherwise learned to live with the gamble.

Weaving, now vertiginous, over to one of the sidewalk tables where couples sit drinking frothy concoctions from glasses that drip with clean, clear sweat, he sets the box down and just before zoning out hears the conversations cease, then resume, now full of loathing.

Gone thirty or forty seconds, more than time enough to appall every last one of them – maybe not enough to ruin their day but lunch hour is shot to hell, because he is fingered by chaos and imperfection and for all they know it may be contagious.

Slowly, then, they readjust, studiously ignoring him, wiping him from awareness. Rendering him invisible: Can't see you, can't hear you, safer for my fragile mind not to know you even exist.

The vintage shop is at the end of the block – inside, a dim museum of mothballed memories and the years, decades, that some people cling to like desperate leeches. Kerry went through a phase last year, wearing the 1930s and '40s on her tall, slim frame. The clothing was authentic, hadn't been cheap, won't be cheap to-morrow hanging on the racks again.

It's his first time in here and will be the last. The woman who owns the place – her hair is a shelf-life shade of blonde, cascading with Godiva waves, and she has a toned body but a little wizened face like a monkey's, filigreed from chin to hairline with cracks and creases, same as the otherwise taut arms emerging from her sleeveless top.

He doesn't want to watch those parchment hands as they stroke and paw and reclaim Kerry's noirish year, so he turns away to find whatever diversions he can on the walls, but there's no escape – a few framed pictures leaping out at him, the same woman long before her trampling by crows, production stills autographed to her by the people she's sharing them with, most of them dead but he's forgotten they'd ever been alive. He can feel her about to look his way so he diverts again, anything better than hearing her story of how thirty years ago she was in two or three pilots for television shows no one but trivia hounds know about.

Garrett used to be on TV too, just doesn't feel the need to broadcast old news.

"Now *this* is lovely," she says, and he has to face her.

From the bottom of the cardboard box she's pulled a cameo box handed down from Kerry's grandmother, a tarnished brass oval with carved ivory set into the lid. The sort of keepsake that's among the last things anyone ever sells, because it's one of the first anyone ever owns.

The woman opens the lid to expose the velvety maroon cavity, faded by decades and worn smooth by a hundred thousand moments of jewelry going in, out, chased by groping fingers.

"If they could only talk. Everything they absorb, year after year." She sniffs the inside, delicately, as though it is a wine cork. "Yours?"

"No."

Exactly what she wanted to hear. "A woman's, then? Younger than you? It was a family heirloom?"

He wouldn't correct her even if she was wrong.

"A pretty young woman. Beautiful...?"

Garrett telling her sure, you've got her number; thinking at least she was beautiful when we came out here and *I* still think so but what do I know. I don't make enough to know anything anymore.

Money changes hands, and like anyone he tends to think that's it, this is both the surface and substance of the transaction. But he's wrong, and every time he is, it reminds him how little anyone out here really knows about where they live and what goes on under its filthy polished gleam aside from drive-by shootings and the grinding of tectonic plates.

His sunglasses, he realizes out on the sidewalk – he's left them inside, on the counter.

And when he ducks back in, he finds the woman sitting on the floor, leaning against the wall. Clutching the cameo box in both hands, pushing it to her wadded-up, thrown-away, unfolded face. She makes eager grunts as she pushes her wet tongue as far into the box as she can. It squirms and glistens; it explores every crevice, every ridge of brass and tiny fold of velvet.

After he watches her long enough to get the idea, her eyes pop open, glaring at him over the lid of the box, then she snarls and turns her back on him, as though he might try to grab it back, and resumes her efforts with a wheeze and a moan, feeding on the leftovers.

Not that there would be much left by now, but she's welcome to whatever she can find, no reason she should be any different from the rest of them, any day of the year.

"Garrett? Are you still there?"

"Still here," he told her. Only this morning? Only just.

"I know how this is going to sound, but could you bring some syringes when you bring the money? Lots and lots of syringes, as many as you can."

And Kerry was right, it was a strange request, syringes nothing that either of them had ever had need of before, or even any particular interest in. But then wasn't that just the heart and soul of L.A.—always a new means of expanding your horizons.

Soon after they had begun the relationship that destroyed his career – so this was years ago – Kerry told him that she'd grown up knowing that she would go to California one day and there would never again be any other home for her but what simmered and sighed beneath a west coast sky. She may have been Boston-born and Boston-bred, but migration seethed in her blood, a time bomb of wanderlust sure to detonate as soon as she ripened into adolescence with its disdain of home and anything else too deadeningly familiar.

Garrett understood. At once. Nearly a generation before, he had been young too, suffused with the same itches and burning his face in the sun to summer soundtracks of Beach Boys' songs that extended cocoa butter promises of immortality and compliant pussy. Garrett thirty-five years old and ostensibly knowing better now how to recognize vacant bullshit myths, just no longer caring when Kerry brought it all back fresh again in wistful saltbreeze exultation, and if she was remarkably adult for seventeen, he supposed that even she needed the sham of some far fantasia glittering beside a different ocean.

With Kerry, though, it really was a matter of legacy, a small historical bud far down her family tree. She was descended from the metalsmith, some multiple-great-grandfather, who'd cast the solid gold spike that had been the last one sledgehammered into place on May 10, 1869, in Promontory Point, Utah, to complete the first transcontinental railroad linking east coast with west. How, then, could she do any less than submit to this manifest destiny? How could he, in the end, do any less than follow?

She had always told him that she never saw him as

simply one more older man in the neighborhood, nearer her father's age than her own, who leered at her across the lawn during the summers. No. He couldn't help but be different because he was, after all, on TV every night. Garrett Keneally at Eleven, at his anchor desk to deliver news of Boston and the tantalizing hinterlands. More than just another neighborhood face. Besides, Garrett, with blue eyes and chisel-jaw dynamics, looked like he still had youth on his side, with none of its spotty crudeness.

Linking hands, they plunged into it, and dear god, the revitalization, the sweet musky moss of her, her newness and her fearlessness and all the futures that lay before her smooth arched feet – he wanted them back. He wanted it all to do all over again.

Soon enough. Soon enough. This was exactly the choice forced upon him after they were discovered, the sort of indiscretion that can kill a marriage, and topple a career balanced on credibility. He had no choice but to give in, even when he knew that not one of those who ran the network affiliate would've passed up the same chance had it been set before their sagging jowls.

Southern California it was. Where else would their age gap raise so few eyebrows? Where else would they blend so well? Where else would anyone care so little – even Roman Polanski could still make money here. Where else might it even be an asset, Garrett now one of those who not only appreciated the aesthetic, but he had reconfigured his entire life just to surrender again to the need and allure and the delicate salty sweetness of unblemished skin only now grown to contain the complete young woman inside.

For the first few months, as she took to the west

coast and peeled away the last of the east, it was like watching the birth of a painting from the potential of its sketch, as brush strokes and luscious oils and the play of just-so light wove their spell. She was meant to be here. He was only the catalyst by which it had happened. The sun gilded her skin and plaited streaks of new color through her auburn hair. By night, he could see only the Cheshire crescent of her teeth as she smiled over his groin.

Some days they would fuck at an open window, Garrett turning his back on the cerulean walls as Kerry balanced her rump on the sill, locking both legs around his hips, the yellow-orange chiffon curtains ignited by the blazing sun, and drenched in this molten light they would cling to each other so furiously that there were moments he would have an impulse to shove with his legs and launch them twelve floors to the street below – let gravity preserve the moment, the fantasy of his being here with her, every second chance at life he ever wanted and he knew he'd never get a third, so why not go out at the peak.

His medications overlooked one day, Garrett otherwise sane and happy to be alive, the seizure enveloped him in its dependable warnings and dumped him onto his knees, Kerry disengaging from his wilting cock as he braced against the windowsill like a praying child.

Outside their apartment, the streets and other buildings and the billboards and every single improvement that his species had brought with it had been taken away. For as far as the diseased mind's eye could see, nothing but sprawling grasslands, a ten-thousand-year-old savannah the sight of which shook him so hard it seemed to rattle bones. Right under their noses and shoe soles, the ghost of something even Africa could no longer dream of being. Beyond a grove of cypress bobbed the great gray humped backs of a herd of mammoths. He watched them only long enough to want them to never leave when they began to shimmer like a desert horizon, and a Jeep Cherokee started to materialize through the transparent barrel ribs of a huge bull. It misted away altogether then, along with the rest of its herd, and he stared after it in awe and in grief, feeling a stirring of hatred for that artery of traffic, driving on their bones.

Kerry found a tissue to wipe the wet slick from his chin.

It had never happened this way before, the slipstream of time flowing the opposite direction. But just because you're epileptic doesn't mean you can't see the past.

"Is Skip still alive?" Garrett asked, daring to, finally. Only this morning? Only barely.

"Is there any reason you think he shouldn't be?"

"I found the test results. In the desk drawer. The day after you left." Garrett listened to her listening to him breathe, both of them knowing that he needn't be in a hurry for any diagnosis of his own. They'd always had a way of sharing the worst. "We're not going home again, are we? Either one of us."

"Oh, Garrett," she whispered. "We haven't really been home for twelve years."

An epileptic with a mission, Garrett spends the afternoon in a way he's never thought would be necessary. Taking their lives apart layer by layer, then seeing who bites, who's hungry for the peelings. Furniture, appliances, clothing, music, electronics – you name it, it's on somebody's menu.

Possessions are for the living.

Until finding Kerry's test results the other day, he felt as healthy as ever. Since then, a morbid resignation has settled over him and he thinks he can sense the invader in his body. Knowledge is power? Not so fast – just as often it's hopelessness, too, in the presence of viral awareness especially. Then again, maybe it's only the power of suggestion causing that pain in the vicinity of his liver. Fat diseased organ, its shape like a deflating football, one of these days it'll be turning his skin yellow.

Ever since that seizure at the window, when the last day of the last Ice Age showed him its ghost, part of him feels as though it has never truly released him. Pulling him back every couple of months to the Page Museum at the La Brea Tar Pits, where he can wander amid the robust skeletons of wolves and bears, sabertooths and sloths. Each visit he stands made small and diminutive by the remains of an Imperial Mammoth, twelve feet tall at the shoulder and how those future freeways must have rumbled beneath its feet. Its brownish tusks are vastly long and curved, tips crisscrossing into a cradle wide enough to lie in.

You weren't born here. You came here from somewhere else, he often thinks. *You came here across a land bridge from another time and world. You came here because there was no place left to go. You came here and on your worst day you were still one of the most magnificent things that ever walked, and you should've lived forever. You came here...and then you died.*

It's opened up so much, that empathy. It has led to so much understanding. Even if it's taken epilepsy to get here, maybe the price still hasn't been too steep. He knows what no one else would even dare to guess, knows the secret of this cracked and fissured earth that was never meant for cities: It is saturated with the bestial rage of extinction. It is fractured by the dying roar from animal throats. It is steeped in blood of giants that drained and rotted in the soil, or was cooked away in hot tar.

And every day, ten million conquerors eating and drinking and breathing a little more of the dregs inside themselves.

And on this last day of his and Kerry's former lives, Garrett stripping them down to their cheapest resale essence and leaving the dross along Ventura and Van Nuys and nowhere else that matters anymore, he can finally tell this city the kind of truth he never could on TV.

News flash: You're welcome to it here. All of it. All of you. You slick wet-haired hustlers waiting at the bus station and you executive producers and every one of you in between, you're no different from each other – a cannibal's a cannibal, no matter what grade of meat he prefers. You live in the place where dreams come to die, but if they'll make money you'll plug them into life support. I'm ashamed of myself for ever wanting to belong, but now, finally, I do. I do. Because now you're in my blood.

He knows there's a reason he's saved the gun for last. Better be, when now it's one of the most valuable things he owns, could bring in a couple hundred dollars. He bought it ten years ago, one week too late to spare Kerry the assault in the center courtyard of their second apartment, and it's never been fired since.

Syringes, she wants – except it's not like either of them have a prescription for insulin or run with the junkies.

But if there's anything L.A. has, it's plenty of pharmacies, and a healthy respect for a pistol in the face, held by a man who knows what he wants.

She started to cry then. Only this morning? Only. Only.

"I'm sorry," she sobbed, "I'm so sorry. It's why I had to go driving up and down the coast for a few days, I just couldn't face you yet," until he shushed her and told her it didn't matter any more, if indeed it ever did.

"I'll see you at Skip's house," he said. "Promise me you won't do anything until I get there."

After his business at the pharmacy is finished, the sun is sinking toward the west in a streaked haze like blood and fire, and the peppery winds sweep the city with the roasting breath of perdition. When Garrett drops down to the Hollywood Hills, the car turns sluggish as the road climbs and winds past prime real estate as cramped as any street in Calcutta. Driving from memory and making a few wrong turns – if you live here, confusion is your best defense against anyone you don't want to see, the paradox being sometimes even the cops get lost when you really want them.

Skip Ackerman's house – he rents – sits abutting the street, and Garrett has barely enough room to park out of the way, along the garage door. One house across and down, a lawn crew is stowing their gear in the bed of a dirty white pickup truck with crumpled fenders.

Three dark-skinned men, laughing, pouring water over their heads. Mexican, he assumes – anybody would – but realizes his mistake when he gets a better look. They're Indian.

He wonders if they have the remotest idea what they are. Shot and shoved across the country a few hundred miles at a time, well, sure, but that's yesterday's agenda. Deeper than that, then – the next wave after the mammoths. They're in good company, at least.

Kerry lets him through the door after he rings the bell a couple of times, then triple-locks it after him. When he closes his eyes as they hold each other he can still feel the slim and hopeful creature she was a dozen years ago, the one for whom he gave up everything and has never gotten it back.

Yet he still has *her*. Against all odds, he still has her.

Days ago, when she disappeared, he had time to think maybe this was it, the accident of love that would rip them in half. He had spent years dreading her awakening – that he would be an old man long before she was an old woman. Now, with any luck, they can die together. It would he hell on her, though, knowing she's the one who brought it home.

But Kerry is the last one he would ever blame. The way he sees it now, this has been a long time coming.

When he pulls away from her arms and brushes the uncombed hair back from her face, out of self-conscious habit she tries to turn her head the way she always does, but this time he won't let her. Wants to see her face, all of it, realizing now that he even missed the scars – two fine red ridges that curve away from either corner of her mouth, all the way to her ears, giving her what some would think looks like a huge Sardonicus smile.

Coming up on her ten-year anniversary of receiving them that night in the apartment courtyard, the assault never solved. Two men and one knife — no rape involved, only disfigurement, so maybe they knew her but probably not. Mistaken identity seemed likely, Kerry on the pool deck after the knife blade had split open her cheeks like apples, the two guys high-fiving each other while they walked away, in no hurry, as if this were just another job with her blood spreading like red fog across the lit blue pool.

"You got them, then," she says, nudging the sack that he set on the floor so they could hug. "Did you have any trouble?"

"Not much, no."

She pulls a sealed box of syringes from the top of the sack, then looks in at the others.

"My god," she says, "you really came through. There must be, what, over a thousand of them in here?"

"At least that."

Kerry smiles then, fumbling with her hair, about to tell him something like he doesn't have to stay, he should leave now, but he shakes his head and touches a finger to her lips. Save it, too late for that now.

He's known for hours she doesn't need that many syringes to inject anything. Nobody would.

Garrett picks up the sack and follows her through the house, the sort of place that never runs out of boring white walls and black trim and open, slatted stairways. There are enough framed movie posters to comprise a small gallery, most if not all of them for Skip Ackerman productions. Nothing to brag on, and probably none of them anything you've ever seen — direct to cable and video, cannon fodder for absolute boredom when you'll watch anything, then not even remember it.

Skip's personal assistant for four years now, Kerry has seen only two of his movies all the way through. Couldn't tell you what they're about, either, only that they were loud.

She's got Skip in the main room, a cluttered little cavern with plate glass and sliding doors spanning one wall overlooking the Hill. Probably more impressive by night, shades of darkness sprinkled with lights like an inverted sky, but now, in waning daylight, it just looks like any ragged pit crowned with a haze of air you wouldn't want to breathe if there was a choice.

Skip is facing this view from across the main room, wrists lashed to his ankles as he kneels, leaning against the back of his leather sofa with his neck tied to the railing of the stairs to the second floor. He can sag a bit, shift some of the weight off his knees and to his rump, but she's not left him much. His eyes track Garrett when he sees this first new face all day.

"It's been a couple years, but you remember Garrett, don't you?" she asks Skip. "Back home, he used to do the news on TV, but nobody out here would hire him after somebody back east leaked his medical records. You wanted to meet him until you found out that last part. Remember?"

Skip says nothing, but then, he can't. Garrett wishing Skip could ask him what he does instead, and he'd admit it, that the best he can do now is teach others how to read the news at some third-rate broadcast institute. Yeah, Skip would love that a lot.

Garrett has hated him from afar these years but has learned to temper it to a dull red glow, like the rim over the ocean in the last instants of sundown. He's always known what it takes, some days, for Kerry to keep her job. Skip pays just well enough that losing those checks really would hurt. At least it's infrequent, Kerry says, and he comes quickly. They've consulted a couple of lawyers about suing for sexual harassment, never happy with the results. You want to get realistic about it, that's for other industries, not this one.

The best Garrett can figure it, some men simply like a brush with scars every now and then, as long as they don't have to feel them every day.

"I have to pee," she says. "I've been holding it in awhile."

Garrett steps over to Skip as she leaves, reaches for the gag. She's improvised, clever, stuffed a big lime into his mouth and forced him to bite down. Garrett tugs it free, watches Skip work his sore jaws.

Be honest, you're saying: She could've quit her job whenever she wanted, or Garrett could've forced the issue. So maybe Kerry hasn't really minded all that much, and maybe he hasn't either. A safety valve – that's how he'll look at it. Can't call it adultery, not when they never married, just a mandatory cock on the side to keep them together, because what woman still wants the same man at twenty-nine as she did at seventeen? Sometimes he thinks he stole more from her than she'll ever realize, more than she could ever forgive him for if she did.

Call it lucky, then, that they have another head on which to heap all this blame.

"How old do you think I am?" Garrett asks.

Skip peers at him, owlish, blinking. Not a good-looking guy, but not bad, either; nondescript. His hair is wild and mussed, exposing a balding patch the size of a silver dollar. A dry wound is caked bloody on the side of his forehead where Kerry must've swatted him with something earlier.

"I hate that game, it's always a loaded question." Skip sighs. "I don't know, about like me? Close to forty?"

"I'm pushing fifty."

Skip shows genuine surprise, hasn't shaved off years in the interest of playing the game. "Is that *with* surgery...?"

Garrett shakes his head.

Now it's grudging admiration. "Even better. I didn't know you and Kerry were that far apart."

"You wouldn't, would you. Not now. I don't know how it came about that way, it just did." Garrett looking at the warm lime in his hand, the curves of toothmarks in its skin. "A lot of good that does me now, though."

"So what do you want me to say? 'I'm sorry I gave you both Hepatitis C, I'll never do it again, now can't we all just get along?' Sure, whatever makes you happy, but you and her, you're not the only ones suffering here, buddy."

And Garrett's heard enough already, Skip's remorse about as convincing as most of the actors he hires. Garrett jams the lime back into his mouth and waits for Kerry, and when she comes back downstairs he can tell that she's washed her face and straightened her clothing, and when she kisses him he can taste toothpaste, and then he supposes there's really only one thing left.

Kerry retrieves the first of the boxes, each filled with

one hundred Becton-Dickinson five-cc syringes tipped with twenty-five-gauge needles. Skip frowns at first, confused, and after she peels the spike out of its plastic wrapper, he gets nervous. By the time she angles it into a vein along his bound arm, he's trying to squeal behind the lime.

"Quit squirming, Skip," she tells him. "It's just going to hurt more, and if I break a needle off in your arm, does it look like I'm going to run out anytime soon?"

Slowly, as if coaxing the blood, she draws back the syringe's plunger and the plastic cylinder fills with red bright as a ruby. She withdraws the needle and recaps it and sets it aside on the glass-topped coffee table.

Her hand dips into the box for another syringe, strips away its wrapper – "You love L.A. so much?" – and she pierces it into the wormlike vein squiggling across the back of his fluttering hand – "Then let me give you my perspective on it" – and pulls back the plunger – "not that you ever asked my perspective on anything" – and that's five more cc's down – "but now there's no phone and no pager and goddamn you, you're going to pay attention."

Another syringe. Another five cc's drawn from the throbbing vein beside his temple.

"See, this is how L.A. killed me, Skip – "

Garrett, watching her slow, methodical fury, then his stomach knows first, weightless and frustrated, wanting to fly. A flash of light and a sense of unstable ground; the snap of gulls' wings in his ears and a smell like wet limestone in his nose.

" – a tiny little bit at a time."

He weaves away from the escalating panic in Skip's

mad eyes and falls to his knees before Skip's plate glass window on the world, and whatever there will be for him to see. Past, future, either place he goes there's no real time, only their intersection with a now that has outlived its usefulness.

And just look at them up there in that sky, circling in their patient hunger like the black blades of giant scythes.

"What do you see, baby?" she's asking when he comes back. "What is it this time?"

"Condors," he tells her. "Dozens of them. They smell what's coming."

The click of another syringe onto the growing pile.

"Tell them to wait their turn. I got here first."

"Do you still love me?" she asked. Only this morning? Only ever. "Can you?"

"Watch," he said. "Just watch."

It's hours past midnight when they find their way back down out of the Hills, and they've tried to sleep after it was finished but neither of them could, so instead they lay holding each other after this longest day either of them could remember, until they felt rested enough to leave.

South to Sunset, then Santa Monica Boulevard, then west, same as before, same as ever. Always west, always and forever.

They leave the car behind so they can walk the last couple of miles to the beach, and while the final hour of the night is cool, the sand still retains a tiny pulse of yesterday's heat. Thirty yards to their left it's somebody's bed, but ignore them and they go away.

For a while they're content to sit close to the wet boundary where the ocean meets its soft, foaming limit on the shore, as far west as they can go now without drowning. At Kerry's side, the sack, now bulging and irregular, filled with hundreds of capped syringes no longer empty. Soon she drags them the last few feet, then takes them by the fistful and flings them as far out to sea as she can, where they fall glittering like garnets.

Dawn is starting to break behind them when the needles begin to wash up again, like a surf of hospital waste. A new day rolling westward across the land. Boston's been up for hours, but they leave it where it belongs, at their backs, looking out over an ocean meeting a sky still black as tar.

Sea water laps at their feet with its loose cargo. Kerry gives in, reaches down to retrieve a pair of syringes.

"Blood rots first," she says, and he has to ask her what this has to do with anything. "That's why the people who make our bacon are in such a hurry to drain the pigs. Blood always rots first."

She stirs the damp, clumping sand with her toes. Holds up the pair of syringes.

"They make vaccines out of what's already dead," she says.

Kerry uncaps the needles and he accepts the one she offers, and it only takes him a moment to work up enough courage to drive it into his vein and press the plunger home – anything worth a try now, an unconventional cure, or their last chance at belonging out here, truly belonging.

He knows it will not kill them, not today, because the last time he'll see her, Kerry's hair will be blond, yes, but the roots will be growing out, auburn, nothing to have been ashamed of in the first place. Where had she ever gotten the idea it was?

They toss the dead spikes back out to sea, and pretty soon the tide should be going out, so they can scoot a little farther along, waiting for whatever comes next.

The Heart in Darkness
Nancy Holder

"You Americans are so impetuous. All full of derring-do," she said to me and I knew that in that moment my cause, though just, was lost and that she would allow herself to die.

I looked at Catharine, my wife, my soul mate. Her face was the same, her eyes just as blue and clear. She didn't look sick. Ergo, she couldn't be sick.

Couldn't stay sick.

"It's a chance," I insisted, although she had just told me to give it up. But I couldn't give it up. Wasn't I made of the same stuff as John Wayne? Didn't I truly believe that in the eleventh hour, the cavalry would ride in and save us?

"A chance with a success rate of less than five percent." She brushed my hair from my forehead; I wear it long and she's harped all our years of being together that I should have it styled at a shop, turn myself into a grownup. I used to joke to her that I was a film producer and therefore I didn't have to grow up. I could wear jeans and a sports coat and my hair in a ponytail until I didn't have any hair left and I would still command the best booth in the best restaurant in whatever city it was best to be in.

She continued, perhaps to fill in my silence, "Would you really put me through all that for such a slim hope?"

"But it's hope." My fingers gnawed each other. I was the one who felt sick. I was the one who should die, if only of anger and terror and loving her so impossibly too much. "And it's five percent or less. Not what you said. Not less than five percent."

She actually grinned. "Do you know that in Canada, there was a book entitled *How to Cope with Back Pain*, but they had to change it to *How to Conquer Back Pain* to drum up sales interest in the States? No, Jack, it's not for me. I don't want to spend the last six months of my life throwing up what organs I have left."

"Six months to two years." I felt helpless, not against the cancer, but against her passivity. Her willingness to cope with a terminal diagnosis, not to conquer it. Damn it, she should be screaming her denial and making her bargains, not lying among her pillows like Camille, death's odalisque. It was I who had insisted upon the second opinion and the third; I who had used the UCLA medical library and the 'Net to research her disease; I who had asked the oncologist a hundred questions, while Catharine sat in her white paper gown on the examining table. It had been freezing in there; I had demanded a blanket for her. I had told the doctor that I was sorry if he was busy and had a roomful of waiting patients, but damn it, this was my wife we were talking about and I wouldn't leave until we were satisfied.

Until she's cured, that's what I meant; he must have known it. He remained polite and took more time after my tantrum. But then, I am who I am – and you don't get to be who I am by grabbing your ankles with a big smile on your face and letting them do it to you. You claw and you fight and you think odds like five in a hundred are pretty damn good.

But she is British, my beautiful wife, or else it's that she's a woman, or else, that she's been terrorized into paralysis by the word none of us ever wants to hear: cancer.

Catharine has cancer.

It was not a mistake in her chart; it was not a lab mix-up; it was not a script for a Movie of the Week. My darling is horribly ill.

And she wanted to do nothing about it.

Suddenly, more completely than at any other time in our lives, we were separate people. It hurt deeply when she had laughed and said, "You Americans." It was so long ago that we had marveled over our differences, were mesmerized by the apparent uniqueness of each other. You, a woman, me, a man. You, a Londoner, me from L.A. You, calm and placid and expectant, me, impatient and untrusting and a mover and shaker.

Our opposing qualities were appreciated and tolerated in a world inhabited by the two of us and over the years we became denizens with much more in common with each other than with the outside universe. We believed that true love melts individuals, melts boundaries, melts differences.

One goes through life as I, I, I, especially in this

town. Then a brilliant white light pierces your heart and you are we. It is as mystical of a union as the combining of egg and sperm to produce a child, which we never had accomplished, either.

Now we knew why. She had cancer in her sexual parts, but they could cut them out and poison her and irradiate her and when they'd brought her close to death, they could do everything in their power to resurrect her.

Healed.

"Yeah and Sarah Bernhardt practiced being dead by sleeping in a coffin," I hurled at her and I was ashamed. I put my arms around her and sobbed and I was ashamed of that, too. I wasn't the one who was sick. She was. I wasn't the one who'd been handed a death sentence. But if I could changes places, oh, God, I would. Oh, my Catharine, I would. I wouldn't hesitate.

And then I would fight and I would beat that son of a bitch. And we would get on with our lives and our dreams. Make some good films. Make some love. Make some babies.

She held me, saying, "Ssh, ssh. I love you, Jack. It's all right."

"How dare you," I whispered, too low for her to hear. "How dare you say that this is all right."

"Go back to the set," she urged. "There's nothing to do. I called Molly and she's coming over for a while. We'll have some girl time. You'll just be in the way."

For a moment I panicked and then was jealous. I didn't want to spend a single moment apart from her. I didn't want Molly, her best girl friend, to give her anything I couldn't give her. It was a horribly selfish reaction and it lasted only a moment, but I did have it.

Perhaps that was the birth of the shadow.

She kissed me and said, "Go." It seemed a long way to the door, across a floor pitching and yawing like a plane in perilous descent. I left only to please her.

Or did I feel a sense of reprieve, that although our world was collapsing like a burnt-out sun, our outer lives – my outer life – had not yet fundamentally changed? I could walk in the light. I could still go to work, leaving with the belief that she would be there when I got home, ready to hear me rail at the stupidity of the director, the inanity of the script, the immaturity of the actors.

I shut the door and paused on the porch to catch my balance. Our house is in a nice part of Glendale, not a tony and trendy address such as Brentwood or Beverly Hills. I don't mean to boast, but I don't need to prove anything. I could live in a condo in Toluca Lake and drive an old Subaru and everyone in town would chalk it up to some eccentric desire of mine to slum. It would in no way be an indication of how well I'm doing professionally, as the majority of the films I've produced have been blockbusters.

I stood on the porch and breathed in slowly in an effort to calm myself. The geraniums in the stone vases flanking the door were in full bloom, pink and stinky, with light green leaves. The porch, freshly painted, was white and cheery, reflecting the light of the late-morning sun.

I began to walk down the five stone steps that led to the brick pathway that led to the garage.

And as I descended, I noticed an oddly shaped splotch stretched over the street.

It was a shadow.

I frowned and looked up, expecting to see rain clouds. There were none. Then I thought perhaps the sun had moved behind the second story of our house, or of someone else's. But it was arced brilliantly overhead, beaming away.

It was not a shadow, then, I decided, but a splotch after all. Some kind of stain. An oil slick from someone's very troubled car.

I watched my own black shadow as I moved toward the spot.

The other, grayer shape disappeared in an instant.

A plane must have passed overhead, then sped on. I looked up, shielding my eyes from the bright sunlight and saw no jet stream, no plane.

I shrugged, chalked it up to my own internal state and got into my car. I don't have a driver; I don't have a limo. I like to do things for myself.

Some people have teased me that I should have been a director, because I'm a control freak. They assume that directors are the gods of the industry. They're very wrong: producers are. Agents would like to be. But it's producers who bring the pieces together. The producer is the one who says, "Let there be light."

"Then what is the director?" Catharine had once asked me.

"Adam," I told her.

"And who is Eve?"

"The camera."

My job is the distribution of light − upon the moving image, upon the creativity of the assembled talent, upon the script. In a theater, the lights go down and my lights come on. Again, I'm not boasting. That's just the way it is.

On the set – our show had a working title of *Blind Bet*, which is a bet a poker player makes before he sees his cards – things were in a state of minor chaos, which is fairly typical during a production. I smoothed some ruffled feathers, answered a few dozen questions, put in a couple calls and joined the director and his cinematographer for lunch, all on auto-pilot. My mind was back at my house, on the shadow in the street and the shadow that had shown up on my wife's ultrasound.

"Just routine," the doctor had assured us after the miscarriage. "Just to make sure everything's in working order." And then that damn pause. And then, "Oh, what do we have here?"

The illumination of the darkness being the appearance of a shadow in her body.

The metaphor was not lost on me. I wondered if I should call my doctor and have a talk. Get a prescription.

If the shadow returned in the street, I might consider it more seriously.

There was more chaos after lunch. The director was feeling pressured by my presence, but that was his problem, not mine. It was I who had hired him, not the other way around and the set was tantamount to my place of business. My factory, in which he toiled.

I went outside and called Catharine on my cell phone. She was fine. I could hear music on the stereo, heard Molly call a question, my wife's, "Sure, Moll," in response. Catharine sounded completely healthy.

I disconnected the phone and told the director I was needed at home. He tried to look concerned but his relief – like mine earlier – was evident.

I got in my car and left.

The shadow was back.

It had grown. It filled the length of our street. I pulled to the curb and stared at it for five, perhaps ten minutes. No one else drove or walked by, which I found remarkable. While our street isn't a busy one, there is usually some kind of activity during the day.

I wanted to get Catharine, but I stayed in the Rover. Molly's Jag was in our circular drive; I told myself I didn't want to break up the party.

Instead, I drove toward the perimeter of the shadow. In the days of film noir, shadows were painted onto the walls of sets to heighten the sense of tension: the huge, thrown shadow of a hand gripping a knife; the profile of the killer, or of his victim; the canted threshold where death crouched, ready to spring.

As I neared, the shadow disappeared. In one single instant, the darkness dissipated and the landscape lightened as thoroughly and immediately as if someone had turned on a huge reflector.

I pulled in the drive behind Molly and sat, shaking. I was frightened, but I wasn't sure why. I, the so-called master of special effects movies, surely understood about parallaxes and paradoxes, optical effects and optical illusions. Besides, what was a shadow?

On her ultrasound, I thought. On her ultrasound.

I began to cry.

Molly and Catharine tumbled from the entry onto the sunny white porch porch. Their arms were around each other's waists. Molly held a wine bottle and Catharine, a glass. I was alarmed. Should she drink? Was it allowed? I couldn't remember.

"Hey, you!" Molly cried and they smiled blearily at me. They were three sheets to the wind. That was okay, I told myself. It was all right.

I waved at them and got out of the Rover.

The shadow did not reappear that day. Indeed, I forgot all about it. Catharine had a hangover that I mistook for a worsening of her condition and I took her to task for abusing her health and frightening me in the bargain. She was grumpy and said something cruel about her having no health left to abuse and that I needed to come to terms with the truth. One drink, six, a bottle of gin – it didn't really much matter any more.

I swallowed down my hurt and anger, knowing she was beginning to be afraid and planned to stay home that day. But she remembered my lunch with a couple of studio suits and made me go, chiding me as always for my ponytail.

"No one wears ponytails anymore," she said and nearly pushed me out the door.

I drove to Beverly Hills, because suits like to eat there, need to be seen eating there with men like me and as I was turning down Rodeo Drive I slammed my foot on the brake and almost got rear-ended.

The shadow was there; it was enormous, thrown over the facades of several buildings, sliding down the landscaped sidewalks across the broad avenue. It rose into the sky like a barrier of fog.

The car behind me laid on its horn. A woman walking a Jack Russell terrier cried out as the dog jerked free and ran into the shadow. It started screaming; screaming is the only word for it. In agony, it struggled back toward her, as if fleeing and then it crumpled in a little heap.

I watched, astonished. Then the woman ran to it; it crawled out of the shadow and into the sunlight, where it rested its head on her hand.

She turned to me and shrieked, "You bastard!"

I jerked the car forward; I didn't have control. I couldn't get out of the traffic until I was almost at the shadow's edge. Then I pulled to the side and threw open the door, not looking as I stepped out. There was another blare of a horn. I pulled back, then slammed my door and ran toward the woman.

The poor little dog was mutilated. There were large gashes in its side from which blood ran freely, covering the woman's designer suit as she sobbed and held its head. A distinguished gray-haired man was off to the side with a cell phone, saying something about coming right away.

"You bastard," the woman said again to me and the gray-haired man glared at me as if to promise me that once he got off the phone, he would kill me.

I was bewildered. "I didn't, I..." I said. Then, as if it would make sense of everything, I added, "I didn't see him." I pulled out my wallet. "Here's my proof of insurance." The wrong thing to do. This was not a car accident. My business card. "Please, call me," I said. "Please. I'm so sorry."

"Go away." She flailed at me. "Just get the hell away."

I couldn't speak. I just looked at her.

"Goddamn you, go!" she screamed and kept screaming, until the gray-haired man put the phone in his pocket and crouched behind her, encircling her with his arms.

"Haven't you done enough?" he demanded.

I turned and walked back to my car. A number of vehicles had grouped around and behind the accident. Some of the drivers looked on pityingly and some mirrored the fury of the gray-haired man as they watched me climb into the Rover and sit, too upset to move.

"Guilt," I told my doctor. "Survivor's guilt."

"Stress," he rejoined.

Either way, he gave me a prescription for antidepressants and told me to get more sleep. More sleep, as if you can sleep at all when your wife is dying.

When, if you happen to bring home a photocopied article about a new treatment, she shakes her head like a sad Madonna, mother of Christ. Or if you suggest a trip to one of those wellness centers, squeezes your hand and says, "Please, darling, we've spoken about this, haven't we?"

More sleep? It was a miracle I slept at all.

I saw the shadow all the time; I saw birds fly into it and drop to the ground. I saw cats dart into it and collapse.

And then, I saw people walk into it.

But I will not speak of what happened to the people.

And still, no one else saw it. There was nothing about a shadow on the news. There was no investigation of the strange cloud for tabloid TV. There was no Movie of the Week option on it: Shadow of Death. Evil Casts a Shadow. The only talk was of a serial killer who also tortured animals.

I began to wonder if somehow I did, indeed, cause the deaths. If the shadow was really my senses clouding over, presaging a murderous rage. If I had slashed the little dog. If I had shot the birds with a rifle. If I had smothered the cats and if I had done the terrible things to the people that made their last moments so awful to contemplate.

If I was the serial killer.

Everywhere I drove, I saw the shadow. All over the San Fernando Valley, in the hills, in Culver City, where we rented office space and a couple of sound stages. In the special effects houses up by the Jet Propulsion Laboratory.

In Malibu, at parties where everyone remarked on how well Catharine looked, when the truth was, she'd become a walking skeleton. The cancer had spread everywhere; the doctor had no idea why she was still alive. He continued to increase her dosage of pain medication, but in the night, she moaned when she thought I was asleep. She slipped into the bathroom and cried.

The shadow was not been banished by an increased dosage of antidepressants, by a therapist, by a rabbi.

The shadow only gets bigger.

And now, as I sit here on the mountaintop midway between the Griffith Park observatory and the Hollywood sign and look over my town, I wonder, as I have begun to wonder all my waking hours, if the shadow wants something from me. If all this time it has been calling me back into the garden.

Telling me to step into it willingly.

Last night I begged Catharine again to do something. It's almost all I do. I remembered Dylan Thomas: Do not go gentle into that good night.

Oh, my darling, do not go.

She pushed me away, told me that if I don't stop,

she will leave me. She will go away without telling me where and she will die among strangers.

"You really think you are God," she said. I know she was attempting to protect herself, but it cut me to the quick. Can't she see how much I love her? Can't she understand that she's killing me, too?

I wonder why the shadow shows itself to me and no other. Why it allows me – or forces me – to see the pain it inflicts.

Or has it already inflicted pain on us? Is it the thing that gave her the cancer?

I have tried to step into it, but it moves away from me.

But if I surprised it – if I climbed the Hollywood sign – oh, trite cliché! – and jumped – the fallen angel – what would it do?

Would I save the world?

My Catharine?

Or is this a selfish rationale for ending my own pain? For I can no longer bear to see her die in front of me, inch by inch, without a single attempt at treatment. I have begun to hate her for it.

I must decide, for once I climb the sign, I will be spotted. If I waiver, I'll be stopped.

Lucifer was the angel of light.

My heart has become so dark.

Will her last days end in torment, mourning me, remembering that my death occurred after we had quarreled over hers?

Or will I stop her torment if I go? Will it all seem a bad dream? Will she be well again?

Will time run backwards?

Will I ever have existed?

Rage, rage, against the dying of the light.

I stand upon the sign.

The shadow covers the whole of Los Angeles. For all I know, it lies over all of Southern California, of the United States, of the globe. It is a matte, gun-metal gray. It absorbs light, reflects none and yet it is not black.

Perhaps that is what hope does to it.

My impetuous hope, born of John Wayne and full of derring-do. I must have known all along that it would come to this, that I would risk all for her, that I would even risk her.

It's what I am.

It's what I do, or what's a heaven for?

I'm leaping now, my leap of faith. I hear someone shouting, "Don't!"

I made it just in time, then, before I could be thwarted.

And it is cold here in the vast gray shadows. Unbearably frigid. And if this is dying, then dying hurts.

But at least I did not go gentle.

I, at least, have that.

Frayed Seams   Michael D. Fromfelter

The sensation hit me while I was standing in line at Lucky. The lady in front of me, whose perfume smelled like water-soaked rocks, was digging through her purse frantically saying, "I know I put it in here when I left the house. I know I didn't leave it on top of the dresser."

Her checkbook. She had over two full carts of scanned, bagged goods and all of a sudden she couldn't find her checkbook.

She looked up at me and I noticed that she was wearing a wig, a bad wig. The staples in the seamline were showing. "My husband always takes the checkbook out of my purse," she said, hands digging, eyes bouncing from me to the clerk and back again. "He thinks I'm spending money that I don't have." Digging. Digging. "Well, it's just not true!"

Behind me, a kid started screaming. Not crying because Mommy wouldn't buy him any candy, but screaming, like Daddy was taking the whip to his back.

I turned around only because I couldn't stand looking at the Wig-Woman dig through her fucking purse anymore.

The kid was on his knees, pounding his red fists against his mother's legs. Nice legs. I followed them up to the face.

"Got a problem?" the mother asked me, smacking a wad of blue gum. Her thin arms were crossed over small breasts and there were dark sweat stains under the pits of her white T-shirt.

I was about to say something when Wig-Woman screamed, "Here it is!" like she had found the golden fucking ticket.

I turned back around and the sensation hit. I say sensation because it wasn't really a feeling in the true sense of the word. It wasn't like the scene at Lucky was too much to handle and I just snapped, or exploded. No. It was a sensation.

When I turned back to face Wig-Woman I felt like somebody had just crawled in my head and made themselves comfortable. I distinctly remember smelling rotten plums, just for an instant, before a film of light blue shaded my eyes and I tasted salty oranges on the back of my tongue.

The next thing I know, I'm stepping through the front door of my apartment with ice cream dripping out of the box and running all down my arms onto the carpet.

I'm no stranger to blackouts. I've had them on and off for the past seven years. I'll be driving down I-805 on my way to work and suddenly realize that I've been driving on auto-pilot for the past six exits. It's like I get caught up in a thought or a daydream and completely lose track of actual time. I often wonder if I would be capable of responding to an emergency when I'm in the trance. If that Volvo up there lost a rear tire and started snaking back towards me, would I come out of the trance or would I just keep on dreaming until I plowed into the vehicle and created some nasty smears on the highway?

I think I would come out of it. I really do.

But as I stood in the doorway, ice cream dripping cold and sticky down my arm, I began to wonder.

I had somehow managed to get from the line in Lucky, to my apartment (which is a good fifteen-minute drive without traffic), without remembering a thing.

Nothing.

Except the sensation.

Somebody crawling into my head and making themselves comfortable.

Scent of rotting plums right under my nose. Oranges on the back of my tongue.

I ran into the kitchen and tossed the ice cream in the sink, juicy streams of vanilla streaking up to slap the window. I turned on the faucet and ran cool water over my arms, cupped my hands, splashed water onto my face. I remember finding it hard to breathe, like I was having some kind of asthma attack.

I don't have asthma.

The phone rang and that was good. Another voice. Someone I knew, or didn't know that would help me realize that I hadn't stepped into somebody else's nightmare.

I didn't bother drying myself off (I'd have to clean the ice cream out of the carpet anyway). I just ran into the living room and picked up the phone on the fourth ring.

"Travis?" the woman on the other end asked. "Travis, are you there."

I could have sworn I said hello.

"Travis!" A little bit of anger in that voice now.

"Yeah, what's up?"

"I'm at a pay phone downtown." It was Kelly. My girlfriend of one year. Or, as she often said, my wife-to-be. She didn't sound happy. "I don't have time for your games."

"What the hell's wrong with you?" I yelled, getting pissed at the conversation.

"Things have gone to shit down here," she screamed. I heard a bus go by, could almost smell its belching exhaust. Kelly coughed. "My boss has got me running all over downtown looking for a building that doesn't exist. I'm almost out of gas. I'm lost. I'm pissed off, so don't start yelling at me."

I closed my eyes hard. I wanted to yell again...big time. Instead, I said, "What do you want me to do?"

Silence, except for the sounds of the city in the afternoon. "You really don't know do you?" Not anger. Not shock. Just a plain matter of fact tone, like a flatline before the doctor calls time of death.

"Honey," I said, sensing she was going to crawl through the phone and claw my eyes out. "I'm sorry that your day hasn't worked out the way you've planned, but I'm having some troubles of my own over here."

"Our dinner tonight," she said in that same starch tone. "The dinner you planned to make for us for our anniversary tonight."

"Shit," I whispered. But she heard.

"You forgot!" Anger back now, coming strong and red and in my face. "You shit! I'll be late if I'm there at all!" Then the rage and the sounds of the city were all gone because she had hung up.

Kelly and I met last year at this therapeutic outreach program I attended on the advice of my shrink. He said that getting out in the open with a bunch of other basket cases would cause some inner spiritual enlightenment among us all that would help us crawl out from under our dank rocks and shake off the scapegoats of our abusive, brainwashed childhoods so that we might come back into the shiny city and spread our new strength to the less-fortunate parasites clambering through the cement jungle of life.

He didn't actually put it that way, but I knew what he meant.

I didn't want to go. I was just fine working graveyard at the AM/PM, taking my sleeping pills in the mornings when I got home and popping the Prozacs and anafrinills in the evenings. But the shrink convinced me that the trip would be worthwhile. Besides, it was free and I would get to take a week's vacation.

The program was five days long and took place in the beautiful Joshua Tree Desert. Kelly was there on the advice of her parents, who couldn't stand to see her wither away any longer. For years her mother had tried to cure Kelly's anorexia with colorful pills, making her not only thin as a twig but a junkie as well. Kelly's father owned a pharmacy so getting colorful pills had never been a problem.

Kelly and I bonded instantly and spent that week together, inseparable. It had been the first time in almost six years that I hadn't blacked out or succumbed to the panic attacks.

A month later we were living together.

A month after that we bought our first dining room set.

Two months after that she slept with a UPS delivery guy named Dave.

We fought, we talked. I forgave her. She said it would never happen again and that she only did it because she felt confident and sure of herself and wanted to see if other normal people actually found her attractive. I told her that the UPS guy would fuck a box of broken glass if he could find a way to get his pecker into it...and then we never talked about it again.

Now it's our one-year anniversary and I promised her a fresh Italian dinner, which was why I had gone to Lucky.

I looked at the clock.

2:15.

I went out to the car to get the rest of the groceries. I was going to have to do some fast cooking. Or get my ass kicked when she got home.

Halfway through the parking lot, the wind curled up strong and enveloped me with the scent of rotting plums...then the sensation like someone slipped inside my head and made themselves...

wind in my hair... red light yellow light green light go... trees blurring... someone honks... through the front door.. wave.. upstairs second door on the right... dresser... voices whispering... first drawer...

The television's on, a rerun of *Doogie Howser M.D.* I'm sitting on my couch with the remote control in one hand and a photograph in the other. I can smell my secret marinara sauce steaming in the kitchen. I can taste the stale film of bitter oranges on the back of my tongue. My head feels light and empty.

It has happened before, the blackouts. But never like this. Now I'm actually moving, I'm on the go in this state of void.

I look down at the photograph. Kelly and I, hugging each other while standing on a flat orange rock the size of a BMW. Smiling at the camera.

I leap to my feet. Drop the photo. It seesaws onto the coffee table, face up, taunting me.

One of the counselors took that picture on our camping trip.

My mouth is very dry. The scent of marinara sauce is fading.

Kelly still kept that very picture in her old bedroom at her parents' house.

Plums. I smell rotting plums.

She didn't want to bring it to our apartment because she hated how beaten we both looked.

Plums overpowering now, making my eyes water.

"We're not quite finished," said the voice of the person crawling in my head making themselves comfortable...

...blurs... wind... scent of oil and wood... stir the sauce.. add some oregano... clean off the dinning room table and...

I'm sitting at the table cleaning a gun.

I don't own a gun.

I push back in the chair, topple over and crack my head against the wall. The taste of oranges flood my mouth and I gag. Get up quick and stumble into the bathroom, bend over the toilet, and bring up sloppy chunks of hot dogs and fries. I haven't eaten a hot dog in years. I can't remember the last time I had fries. I

smell the plums and bring up another heave, splatter-
ing the toilet seat, flecking my face.

"Not done yet," the voice says, deep and surrounding.

I scream. As loud and hard as I am able. I scream,
and get to my feet, turn on the faucet and splash hand-
fuls of water onto my face. The smell of vomit drowns
out the plums. The sound of my own voice echoing off
the bathroom walls drowns out the voice.

While I can, I run to the phone and dial my shrink.
I look at the dining table as I listen to the phone ring.
The gun is resting on a white cloth, black and oily.

"Come on!" I glance at the clock. 4:30. "Come on!"
The phone rings and rings and rings...

An answering machine picks up.

Plums.

"First things first," the voice says.

Oranges and vomit.

Flash of white light.

I'm standing over the stove, stirring the sauce me-
thodically. My hands tingle.

I spin and puke in the sink.

"What's going on!" I scream at the walls. "This isn't
funny." No one answers. "Okay, I gotta get outta here.
Something bad is gonna happen if I don't get outta here
right now. Just gotta get somewhere to think."

I wipe the vomit off my face, turn off the stove and...

"Delivery time," the voice whispers.

Plums.

Oranges.

Another flash of white light and the sound of wood
being chopped furiously...

I'm stirring the sauce again. I'm wearing the silk

robe that Kelly gave me for my birthday and I'm doused in Drakar, my favorite cologne. My shoulders ache and the taste of oranges has been replaced with bitter copper.

I take the spoon out of the sauce, tap it three times on the edge of the pot, set it down on a folded white napkin.

"Okay." Time to get calm and rational. "Okay." I take in a few, deep breaths and exhale slow and calm. My body feels beat, like I just ran the Boston Marathon. Sweat trickles down my forehead. "Okay..."

My shoulders are alive with pain. The muscles feel compressed, tired, worked. I notice a rash on my right hand between my thumb and forefinger.

"Time to trot," the voice says.

"Wait...." The room blurs. "Wait."

"No time for waiting, Travis." A mocking voice.

"Hold on!" I have to do something. Yelling and denying is getting me nowhere.

Plums.

I watch the sauce bubble, spit, steam.

Oranges.

I remember the gun, cold on the dining room table. The world bends.

"Party time," the voice whispers.

Quick, I jam my hand into the boiling sauce. The pain isn't too bad, cold actually, like my fist was just slammed between blocks of ice.

"That's gotta hurt," the voice says.

I spin around and douse my throbbing hand under cool water. The sauce sluices into the drain, red, disgusting.

"If I did that," the thing in my head continues, "I'd

be screaming bloody murder." He laughs. I imagine him reclining on billowy gray matter and kicking his feet up on my frontal lobe. "Bloody murder." Laughs again, a raspy, chilling sound. "You really have no idea how ironic that is, do you, Trav?"

Pain flaring in my hand now. Nice and hot. Nice and real. Nice and...

"Real, Trav? What? Do you think you're dreaming?" His feet come down and I feel soft, uncomfortable pressure on my brain stem as he stands. "You've got a reason for everything, don't you?" He has an ugly face, deformed somehow. His spine is lumpy and contorted. "So I ain't pretty," he admits, pacing slow. "You never even cared to notice my face before."

I watch the water pour over my swollen, blistered hand. I concentrate hard on the pain.

"That's definitely gonna leave a mark." He leans against wall of brain tissue.

I look at the clock on the microwave.

5:30. Kelly will be home in an hour and I am having a complete mental collapse in the kitchen. I have also managed to lose about three hours of real time.

"Don't even start bitching about how time flies, Trav." He starts pacing again, moving graceful through slimy coils of gray matter. "This is the most time you've given me in I don't know how long."

I feel nauseous. If he was in my guts I'd stuff my bleeding hand down my throat and try to puke him out.

"Putting a burn like that under running water is about the worst thing you could do. You're supposed to wrap something like that up in a loose bandage and call nine-one-one." He makes a tsk-tsk sound. "Guess I must've been the one awake during that first-aid class."

"Fuck you..." I mumble.

"Ah!" He raises his arms. "The almighty speaks." He bows. "I'm honored that you finally acknowledge me."

"Fuck you," I groan to my hand. If I talk to him, I'll finally have gone off the edge. The wagon will come, big guys, white smocks, leather straps, heavy sedation. Actually, heavy sedation might not be such a bad...

"You're already over the edge, Trav. It's too late for straps and medication." He laughs. "Wait until you see what you've done."

"What?" I ask, giving in. I try to hear the hiss of the faucet, the hum of the refrigerator. I hear only wet sucking sounds as he traverses barefoot over mucus coral.

"We were doing fine," he says. "You and I against the daily grind. Those meds you were on kicked ass. I had some great hallucinations. Didn't even have to bother you much, except when I got antsy."

"Who are you?" I ask, rotating my hand, watching as the flowing water ripples over blisters and slimy tissue.

He laughs. "I'm you, idiot. What did you expect me to be? A demon?" He brings his hands up to his distorted face and wiggles gnarled fingers. "Satan!" That laugh again. "Maybe that shrink wasn't full of shit after all. You do have a problem claiming responsibility."

"You're not me..."

"Oh yes. I am. You divided us, but we're two peas in a pod. Two nuts in a shell."

"What have you done?" I don't want to know, really. Just want to go to sleep.

"What have you done? I'm much too small to be more that an itch in somebody's eye. You're the one with the strong arms and...itchy trigger finger."

"Oh my god..."

"Too late to play innocent now. They'll fry you for this. The ax, by the way, was completely your idea. I told you it was too cliché but you wouldn't listen. I said we could have been more creative."

"Oh my god!" My stomach knots, twists, lurches.

"You did it to yourself. Had to go and fall in love with that basket case. You did this, Travis. YOU!"

I back away from the sink.

"It's in the living room," he says.

My hand is alive with pain. Real pain.

"If you let me handle the situation from here," he offers, "we might be able to get this right."

I nod. With what little strength I have left, I nod. I keep nodding until the room begins to bend...

I took a steak knife out of the drawer and headed into the living room. Headed! Ha! The pain in my hand was stimulating, borderline erotic. I might do the other one later if I could find the time.

The box was on the coffee table, UPS-sealed, of course. The bottom was stained dark but none of the blood had seeped out.

Very cliché. Head in the box was the oldest trick in the book.

I cut the tape off the box and opened the top flaps. His hair was thick and easy to weave my fingers into. I pulled his head out and kicked the box off the table. I took a good look at the jagged, meaty tissue of his neck. That ax did some serious damage. That's why my shoulders were killing me. His throat was a mess. No matter. I was just going to have to accept the fact that this evening wasn't going to turn out perfect.

I looked at the clock.

5:50.

Time to work.

I sat on the couch and held his head in my lap. I worked with the knife carefully, tediously, carving the single letter large enough to make a statement without completely defacing the guy. After all, if she didn't recognize him right off, all of my hard work would be pointless.

The hardest part came when I had to peel the letter of flesh off his face. I had to make sure that it came off in one piece. I had to do a little more cutting to get it just...right.

I threw the useless wad of flesh on the carpet next to the spilt ice scream and took in my work of art.

A perfect, bloody K now crisscrossed the guy's face. Over the left eye. Down the cheeks. Up across the bridge of the nose. I was able to peel off a few jagged strips of skin to smooth up the edges of the letter.

K for Kelly.

K for kunt.

Perfect.

Visceral.

Unmistakable.

My point would be clear and concise.

I carried the head over to the table, got the gun and returned to the couch.

6:30.

I set the head beside me on the couch. But something was not quite...

Ah! I spotted his work cap on the floor, flecked with blood. I brushed off what I could then placed the hat on his thick hair. Much better.

I gripped the gun sturdy and strong and waited for my lovely Kelly to walk through the front door.

Backwards . . .

Parallel Highways

James Van Pelt

The semi-trailer truck's rear tires rumbled a yard from Jack's window. A faded sign in red, HORIZON TRANSIT, in giant letters, decorated the trailer. In the rear mirror, another eighteen-wheeler's grill loomed just off the bumper, and in the right lane a line of cars slid by, no more than a half a dozen feet between them.

White knuckled, Jack gripped the wheel. Backwash from the semi rattled his little car, and he fought the tug that pulled him toward the tires spinning to his left. Blurred at the tip, the speedometer needle hung just beyond eighty miles per hour.

"He's coming over," said Debbie. Her voice cracked. From the corner of his eye, Jack could see she'd balled a handful of skirt into her fist. She sucked in a breath, as if she were about to scream, but instead she murmured, "He's coming."

"I can see," he snapped.

The semi's trailer of ribbed aluminum, rivet studded and coated with dust, crossed the line, narrowing the space. In the truck's mirror, dark glasses hid the driver's eyes, but he seemed to be looking right at them.

Jack whipped a glance over his shoulder. The other semi behind them had moved up, now nearly touching their bumper. No break in the line of traffic to his right, but he signalled anyway, stomped on the accelerator and slid over, hoping for a gap. Traffic behind him, stretched in a domino row of glaring windshields, and he realized no one was going to let him in. They *couldn't* let him in.

Inexorably, the truck closed the distance, squeezing the lane.

"Oh, no," Debbie moaned.

"I've got it," Jack said. "I've got it."

He dumped into fourth gear, winding the car's little engine into the top of its RPMs; it jumped forward. They passed the trailer's front wheels. A woman in a beat-up station wagon on their right leaned on her horn, flipping them off, but she moved over a bit, and so did the Volkswagen in front of her.

Jack scooted close to them, crossing the lane stripes, passing the station wagon, the semi's wheels roaring in his ear. He juked the car right, bumping the Volkswagen; metal crunched, and Debbie fell against him, her chest heaving, her arm slippery with sweat.

The face in the Volkswagen contorted in anger and fear.

Better you than me, Jack thought. Although his car was small, he knew the Volkswagen didn't have any weight at all. If he had to, he could force himself into its spot in the traffic.

Now, horns all around them blared. Traffic in front
of them rippled. Tail lights flashed. A pickup that had
been blocking the Volkswagen cut left in front of the
semi, and the its air horn erupted, but now there was a
space to the right.

Sobbing, Jack pulled in front the Volkswagen, clip-
ping its bumper on the way, and another opening appeared on his right, which he took.

Two lanes separated them from the trailer-truck,
now bombing along as if nothing had happened. Jack
pried a hand loose from the steering wheel and wiped
his mouth. His chin was slick.

He checked the mirrors. As far back as he could
see, traffic. The highway faded into the blue distance.
Same in front. One more lane over, a cement retainer
separated them from the city, a numbing series of dirty,
grey warehouses.

He took deep breaths, letting himself calm down.

"Missed us that time," he said, and he tried to laugh,
but it came out tight and fake, like it felt.

Debbie sat up straight, smoothing her skirt over her
legs. She looked out the side window, pressing her hand
against it. Long brunette hair with just a hint of a curl
at the end brushed her shoulders. Her face reflected a
little in the glass. Deep, brown eyes. No makeup. A
serious woman carrying despair in the lines of her
frown.

Beyond, building after shadowless building rolled by.
The sun stood exactly overhead, but smog or mist
fuzzed away its outlines, so the sky glared hot, white
and without form.

"We should have let that car in," she said.

"Which?" He knew what she was talking about. It

was an old argument.

"We shouldn't have been in such a hurry."

Jack checked the mirrors again, then closed the distance between him and the next car to get the guy following him off his tail.

She said, "I don't recognize anything."

"I know."

"It could be L.A." She looked at him without moving her hand, her eyes so tired that they appeared as if they'd been punched.

"Or Pompeii."

"That's not funny."

"It's a superhighway from somewhere. Just as well could be Pompeii. Or maybe Rome, just before Nero burnt the sucker."

"Stop it."

"Do you think there was a freeway between Sodom and Gomorrah?" He laughed a little easier this time but bitter.

"Sodom and Gomorrah," she said, "L.A. What's the difference?"

"If it were L.A., we might be able to get off. Merge lane," he said. Whatever the junction was, a spray-painted white hand obscured the name. "Should we take it?"

"I thought that was Anaheim we passed yesterday," she said wistfully. "I always liked Disneyland."

"I'm taking it."

Jack scanned his left, tapped the breaks and eased into a space between a Bronco with tinted windows and a guy on a motorcycle. The cyclist's head wove back and forth as if he were listening to a private symphony. Hair spilled out beneath his faded bandanna and streamed in the wind. Ahead of them, taillights blinked and cars jockeyed for position.

Traffic split, and Jack followed the curve of the road beneath an overpass. A green highway sign said, *Carmilhan — 76 miles*. Within a few minutes, the warehouses disappeared, replaced by desert and twisted Joshua trees streaking by behind the concrete retainer.

Jack sighed. Highway reached before him straight to the horizon as unwavering as a knife edge. Here, the cars spaced themselves a bit. Twenty to thirty feet between them, but the asphalt still whined under the wheels at a steady eighty miles per hour. He laid his head back and stared at the ceiling for a second, then blinked hard and rubbed his hand across his eyes.

"I'm exhausted. Can you handle it for awhile?"

Debbie nodded, moving next to him, onto the emergency brake. She put a hand on the wheel and arched up as he slid underneath her, the back of her blouse wet with perspiration. Now, almost sprawled across the seat, the brake's handle digging into his back, he kept a foot on the accelerator. She stepped over his legs, careful to keep from turning the car with her hip as she dropped into his place.

"What should we do at the next junction?" she said.

Jack reached into the tiny backseat for a jacket, folded it over several times, then wedged it into the corner between the top of the seat and the doorjamb. He rested his head on it and closed his eyes. Humming wheels whipping over road whispered against his cheek. "It doesn't matter," he said. "Go where you want."

Speed varied as Debbie adjusted for the traffic. Air rushed past the window, whistling a little in some crack he'd never been able to find. After a while he drifted into a kind of false-sleep, not quite dreaming, not quite aware of where he was, and he felt like he was floating. Then he said, or thought he said, or maybe even imagined he said, "How come all roads lead everywhere, but you can't get there from here?"

Debbie didn't answer, so he decided he hadn't actually said it, and he let the car's motion lull him further. He thought about treetops waving back and forth and a time when he rested beneath them, watching diamonds of sun coming through the leaves. All he wanted was to sleep and to wake up there – to wake up anywhere other than on the highway – not to be pounding out the miles and watching the bumper in front of him. Jack wanted to sleep and to wake up and to sleep again far away from the road and horns. Far away from the zombie motion of driving the car.

He lurched, bouncing his forehead against the glass. No telling how long he'd been asleep. It didn't feel long. He squinted against the pain, then peeked over at Debbie. Her chin was down, eyes closed; her hands loose on the wheel.

Too late, he jolted upright, reaching for her. Concrete whizzed inches from his side window. Metal screeched. Sparks fired from the front of the car. Debbie shot up. Overcorrected.

The world keeled over and slowed as the car went sideways and rolled. Jack floated to the ceiling as it crumpled toward him. Glass shattered into the passenger compartment. His arm broke first, a wet snap above the elbow, then his shoulder. Then he hit the ceiling. And last, as the car rolled, he saw through a red veil the semi bearing down, an avalanche of metal

JAMES VAN PELT   193

and momentum.

*   *   *

Jack's consciousness surfaced in the half-death in a white flash of agony, and through the shock he thought, pain slows time. Agonizing second after second. He thought, terminal cancer victims must hear clocks in their blood slowing down. Any minute and every minute an infinite reach. Unstoppable and dispassionate. Waves lapping against the sand. Everyone like the first; none the last. All bones crushed. All flesh mangled. Pain living forever. All of it over and over again. For infinite time, his bones broke one after another, and like Prometheus, without healing and without cessation, the bones broke again. He had no way to tell, nothing to measure it against, but the crash seemed to replay for a thousand years.

*   *   *

"I'm sorry, Jack." Debbie held the wheel in one hand and touched herself with the other. First, her face, then across her chest and onto her leg. "Oh, god, I'm sorry."

They passed under another sign, *Carmilhan – 8 miles/Alice Mar –104 miles/Titanic – 156 miles*. On the dunes beyond the cement retainer, isolated Joshua trees spaced themselves between long patches of bare sand. Each like a mutant sentinel, holding mutant limbs to the brilliance of the white sky.

Jack felt his own arms, stretched his back. Nothing broken. Nothing even sore. "It's inevitable," he said. "It's not your fault. We're bound to get tired."

She shook. Her hands trembled on the steering

wheel. "I can't do that again. It's not fair that I should have to do that again."

Cars bunched up in front of them, closing the distances. Looking in the mirror, Debbie switched lanes, away from the congestion. In a minute, they passed a four-vehicle pile-up, two cars, a cement mixer and a bread truck. Broken glass crunched under their tires as they went by. Debbie looked away.

"Dying's the best rest I get," said Jack. "It's a silver lining."

"I don't know why we get sleepy. We don't eat. We don't go to the bathroom. The stupid car never needs gas!" Debbie said, her voice on the edge. "You know what else? I don't see enough accidents. If everybody's like us, then there ought to be accidents constantly. There are people all by themselves in half the cars. Who gives them a rest? But most of the time, traffic's moving. Why is that?"

"Well, if we're logical . . ."

"You're not a scientist anymore! I'm not a student in one of your classes. Nothing's logical about this!" Debbie's lips paled; her face was so tight.

Jack touched her arm. "It's O.K. It's just conversation."

She took several shaky breaths, then relaxed. For a second, Jack saw in her face a semblance of his wife the way she was aeons ago, when they climbed in the car and left for the commute. They'd been uptight; they'd argued; they were late; it was her fault; it was his fault. He'd cut into the traffic viciously. Someone beeped at them; then they'd settled into the flow, and she'd relaxed, just for a second, like she did just now.

"Not logic, then," Jack said. "Thinking it through,

though. If there are solitary drivers, and they're like us, then they ought to be crashing left and right, but they don't. So they're not like us."

"I guess we know that."

Jack peered into the car beside them, a shiny, blue Lexus. Inside, a man in a business suit stared straight ahead. Lots of commuters looked like him, focussed in a kind of catatonic way. Locked on the road, frozen into position as if posing for portraits. Lost in their thoughts, he supposed.

But some of the cars that passed . . . the occupants weren't possible . . . were painful to see. He noticed that Debbie had quit looking long ago. But how often do we really see the people in the other cars on a commute? thought Jack. Maybe the highways had always been like that. Maybe I never paid enough attention. He had a theory that this is the way it had always been: traffic consisted of demons, civilians, newbies and the damned. Sometimes it was mostly civilians: drivers who got on the highway, went somewhere and got off, never knowing what drove beside them. Sometimes it was mostly the damned, like them, who died and lived and kept on driving. Sometimes there were newbies: the damned before they died the first time. And then, there were demons. Jack shuddered thinking about the sunglassed face looking back at him in the semi's mirror. That driver had known they were there, but he came over anyway.

Jack said, "We have to sleep, or we'd go insane, and if we were insane, this wouldn't be so bad."

"You're assuming we're being punished."

"It's like the fate of Sisyphus. He pushed that old boulder to the top of the mountain in the Greek underworld, but it wouldn't stay there. So his curse was to walk after the thing and roll it back up. If he only had to roll it up, and he could never stop, he'd never have time to think about his sins, but the rock rolled down, and he'd go after it. The punishment was in the walk down, while he was resting. We've got to sleep so we can wake up and realize again what our task is. It's our walk back to the boulder."

"So are we wimps or heroes?" said Debbie. "Are we resisting our fate or giving in?"

"Well, I guess if this were a movie, we'd be wimps. We're not solving our problems. But in real life sometimes the most heroic thing you can do is to stay even and not give up. So we're heroes."

"I don't feel like a hero. I haven't done anything."

Debbie let her hands slip to the bottom of the wheel. She was steering with the tips of her fingers barely draped. Back in the Joshua trees, a black shape moved; Jack only caught a glimpse of it. It was like a bear, but its arms were loose-fleshed, hairless and yellow. It looked up from whatever it was feeding on. Eyes glinted.

"We're not in our world," he said.

"I'm sure that was Anaheim the other day. Maybe we're there part of the time. If we could find our way back."

"One freeway to another. Merge lanes and junctions – there's never an exit."

"I remember the signs: Hermosa Beach and then Long Beach. We were going west on the 91. Maybe these are like parallel universes, except they're parallel highways. Part of the time we cross over. Do you think anybody saw us? Do you think we looked different?"

Debbie drove for three hundred miles before they switched. She rested her head and closed her eyes immediately. Ahead, a line of hills rose out of the desert, and soon he was climbing steadily. Joshua trees gave way to pinion as the road wove higher and higher. Occasionally he passed a camper or heavy truck laboring in the right lane, belching out exhaust. A sign read, *Slower traffic keep right: No stopping on the shoulder.* He smirked. They'd tried stopping twice, pulling against the cement retainer, only to watch the following traffic pile into them, as if they were incapable of stopping themselves. The second time they'd burned. A thousand years in the fire.

Once he'd seen a man jump from a car; maybe he was a newbie, desperate to escape the road. The man slowed as much as the flow allowed – maybe fifty miles per hour – then opened his door and rolled out. Jack had been three cars back, and passed him as he slid and tumbled on the asphalt. Craning his head over his shoulder, Jack saw the man, amazingly, stagger to his feet just before a bus creamed him.

No stopping on the shoulder, Jack thought. No kidding.

A road sign read, *Mary Celeste −14 miles.* "That's a phantom ship," he said. Debbie turned on her seat; opened her eyes.

"What?"

"Sign said, Mary Celeste. It's a ship whose crew never made port. They found her floating around, perfectly seaworthy, but no one on board."

"I know about the Celeste," said Debbie, her eyes closed again. "We're more like Vanderdecken."

"Who?"

Debbie covered her face with one hand. Jack couldn't tell if she were crying or not. "Vanderdecken captained the *Flying Dutchman*. During a storm he swore an oath that he'd sail around the Cape of Good Hope or be damned forever."

"What does that have to do with us?" said Jack. He could feel the anger welling up inside him. She's always bringing it up, he thought. She can't give it a rest.

"We should have let that car in. You shouldn't have said, 'Damned if I'll let someone cut me off this morning!' They died because of you." Her voice wasn't angry, but it was flat and tired, as if announcing news she'd accepted long ago.

His heart pounded in his ears. She won't leave it alone, he thought. It's always my fault. He remembered the morning this started, holding his own in his lane, the early commute streaming toward its destination, when he saw the mini-van coming toward him from the on-ramp. He'd measured its speed, watched it, and saw that it was going to merge in front of him. He was in a hurry. He was edgy in that special manner that driving in traffic made him. The mini-van approached. Jack would have to give way to let him in. "Damned if I'll let someone cut me off this morning," he'd said, and he smashed the accelerator. For a moment, the mini-van paralleled them, the driver leaning to his left, searching for a break in traffic.

He must not have ever seen the broken-down car on the shoulder. Jack didn't until the last second, just a glimpse of a jack holding up the driver's side rear, of a tire laying on the road, of someone on his knees holding a lug wrench. Then the mini-van plowed into the parked car.

Jack pictured the crash. "I don't want to talk about it. I don't even want to think about it anymore." He heard his voice straining.

Debbie didn't say anything. Curves held Jack's attention for a moment. The road had gone to two lanes, and he had to concentrate on driving. Then, the hills opened up, and the ocean spread out before them. The highway fell toward the sea. Soon they were driving a road that held close to cliff edges overlooking stony places where waves lapped dully against kelp-encrusted rock. Even through the window, he could smell the salt and rot.

Then Debbie said, "I would have done the same thing, Jack. I wouldn't have let the van in that morning."

Jack remembered the smoke from the accident. As they had driven on, a pillar of smoke had risen behind them, climbing into the sky like an angry spirit, black and red and writhing.

The memory of smoke clear in his mind, he drove on.

They stayed on the coastal highway for 3,700 impossible miles before a car coming toward them crossed the lane, catching their side, driving them off the road, over the cliff, tumbling against the rocks for five hundred feet. The last thing Jack heard was water hissing against hot metal. Then the sea rushed into the car.

*   *   *

No one knows about pain but those who are in pain. Only the hurting know what it is. Memory of pain is not pain.

Description of pain is not pain. Small hurts are not like great ones reduced. True pain lives in the ever-present moment, expecting nothing, owing to nothing, overwhelming all other thoughts. For a thousand years, Jack tried to scream. Water filled his lungs. Everything was broken, and he was always drowning.

*   *   *

"You were saying?" said Jack, trying to sound as if nothing had happened, as if no time had passed, but Debbie didn't answer. For the longest time she kept her face to the window, so that all Jack could see was the back of her head. He turned inland at the junction to Palatine and soon the lanes multiplied and they were in city traffic again.

"Our driving record sucks," she said finally. "They should pull our driver's licenses." She started laughing, and it built on itself, an insane-sounding layering of laughter until Jack couldn't tell if she were laughing anymore or shrieking, and it scared him. After minutes of this, she quieted down, although every once in a while, she'd chuckle, and Jack was afraid she'd start again.

She said, "You know what I'm thankful for?" She paused a half beat. "That we don't have to pay car insurance anymore. It's just a relief." The chuckle came out of the back of her throat, and she wiped tears from the bottom of her eyes.

Jack drove for twenty hours straight, 1,600 miles before switching. Mostly they passed through baking desert, their air conditioner battling vainly against the heat pouring in; the glare off windshields stabbing his eyes, but every once in a while, buildings would loom up on either side, warehouses, factories, strip malls, and he could read the signs: AAMCO, QUIZNOS, BIG O, WINCHELLS, AMERICAN FURNITURE WARE-HOUSE, WAL–MART. Sometimes he couldn't read the signs; they weren't in any language he recognized. But never an exit, just junctions. Highway leading to highway; concrete bridges twining over, under and around each other, filled with cars streaming end to end.

Their drivers studied the road with the peculiar dead look of the long-distance traveler. In some cars, the passengers slept. In some they read books. Jack saw kids and old folks and dogs, all closed in, all isolated in their eighty-mile-per-hour fish bowls. And in some cars he saw monsters.

Debbie covered almost nine hundred miles before giving Jack a turn, and he went for 1,300 more. They switched a dozen times, often times saying nothing for hundreds of miles; often times both awake, watching the road unreel before them.

A low set of hills shrugged up on the horizon, and soon they wound through dry, grass-covered slopes. For miles, rows of giant windmills lined the hills, their huge, high-tech blades spinning in a wind they couldn't feel in the car. Then they passed the last windmill and other highways joined theirs, adding a lane or two each time. Jack was driving when they rounded a curve and a great city sprawled in the vast valley below. Through the haze, as far as he could see, rooftops and roads, and the traffic drew them in.

Something touched his hand on the emergency brake. He looked down. Debbie's hand rested against his, and he took it, pressing his fingers between hers. They drove into the city hand-in-hand.

Debbie scrutinized the buildings as Jack eased from one lane to another, always on the lookout for potential trouble. His back ached; his eyes burned with weariness.

"It's L.A. again," she whispered. "We're on the 10."

"They all look the same," Jack said, but he noticed the palms growing beyond the retaining wall and the manzanita in the median. "I haven't seen a sign."

"I think it's L.A."

"I hope it isn't. I couldn't stand it if we were this close." But he sat up more in his seat, a little less tired.

She squeezed his hand. Malls flowed by and R.V. lots. Trucks filled the road: tankers, movers and the semis. Cars darted like smelt among the shark, moving around their ponderous bulk, giving way, sliding over, clearing a path. In the distance, a series of high rises peeked out of the haze.

"I remember audio-books," said Debbie. "If you weren't with me, I could start one in the morning and finish it on the way back. I used to think my commute was half a book long."

"I didn't know that. For me the drive was time to get good thinking done. From Banning to San Bernardino I'd formulate the problem. From there to Pomona, I'd come up with various approaches, and by Pasadena I'd have the day planned out."

The traffic flow varied. Cars slowed and came together for miles, crawling at fifty or sixty miles an hour. Then, without any perceivable reason, they would speed up and spread out. Jack thought of it as "accordion traffic," and it took all his attention. Now he drove with both hands on the wheel, watching for the sudden cut, keeping out of others' blind spots. Drivers looked tense and focussed. They snapped glances in their mirrors; kept a thumb near their horns. Blinkers flashed. Cars vied for placement as junctions came up every mile or so.

Jack changed lanes twice to get into position for the Santa Ana junction. It *was* L.A. he decided. Maybe a parallel one, but L.A. just the same. He could get them to Anaheim at least. Debbie could see something familiar before they followed the road back out to alien landscapes and meaningless junctions that led them nowhere at eighty miles per hour.

He could get them to Anaheim.

Traffic flowed slightly faster in his lane. They crept up on cars, taking minutes to pass them. A semi to their right, ahead of them, blocked the signs. Jack wanted the Compton junction that would take them west on 91, but he didn't know if he needed the left or right side of the highway. A sign blinked by, and he missed what it said.

Slowly they closed the distance. The semi's wheels roared by Debbie's window, and Jack suddenly got scared. Everything felt the same as it had once before. He'd heard these tires before.

"What's that truck?" he asked, voice tense.

Debbie pushed her face to the window and read the side. "Horizon Transit, why?"

"Jesus," said Jack. He couldn't see the driver's face, but a leather-clad arm rested on the driver's door. Only a few feet separated Jack from the car in front of them, a green lowrider with maroon tassels dangling in the rear window.

Jack tapped the top of the steering wheel. Two lanes of cars to his left were packed solid, hardly a hand's breadth between them. No chance of cutting over and away. All he could hope for was that nothing would happen, because there was nothing he could do to protect himself.

At mid-trailer, the truck's turbulence buffeted them and pulled them over. Jack leaned on the wheel, keeping them in the center of their lane.

Debbie said, "That's the same one, isn't it."

Howling, the trailer's front wheels passed the window in a blur of rubber and spinning metal. They were beside the cab. Jack could see the foot rest and the bottom of the door. Then they were by.

Closing his eyes for a second, Jack breathed easier. The lane to their right was now open for a hundred yards, as if no one wanted to be in front of the semi. Keeping one eye on the truck in his mirror, Jack scanned the road ahead for junction signs. He couldn't remember how long he needed to stay on 57 before hitting 91. It seemed like years since he'd driven this stretch of road. Years of driving and driving and driving, but never arriving.

After minutes more, they caught up to the car that was immediately ahead of the semi, now a hundred yards behind. Jack kept looking for the signs as they inched past.

"Oh," said Debbie. "That poor man."

In the car beside them, a yellow Volvo sedan with two little boys in the back seat, the driver was wide-eyed and weeping. The man rotated his head left and right, and Jack could see in his face disbelief and growing horror.

A newbie, Jack thought, and he remembered when he and Debbie realized they were trapped, how the sickening dread had welled up inside them. The traffic wouldn't let them stop; there was no place to exit, and they were trapped. They must have looked like this.

The man's face was pure anguish. He didn't even appear to see Jack and Debbie looking in at him, and in the backseat the children played, two little boys with their heads down studying something between them, maybe a coloring book.

What could they have done to deserve being here, Jack thought, and the image of the children waking up in the half-death after their first inevitable crash boiled up within him. A thousand years (it seemed) of pain and death. What could they have possibly done?

Tears glistened on the man's face. He barely seemed to be paying attention to the road as he wandered from side to side.

Jack felt a fist in his throat. He couldn't take his eyes away from the man. Then the car behind Jack beeped, a short angry beep that said, "Keep up, buddy. You're slowing me down." A gap had opened in front of Jack.

He checked his rear-view mirror. The driver behind beeped again, but what Jack saw was the semi closing fast. The hundred yards was now fifty. Black exhaust streamed from the truck's twin pipes above the cab, and the windshield glared like a rectangular sun. Directly in front of it, the unknowing newbie waited to be squashed. He didn't see the traffic. He didn't see anything, and his boys played on.

Debbie saw it too. She looked at Jack.

Their eyes locked, and hers brimmed with sadness.

Twenty-five yards back, the semi leapt eagerly. It growled in triumph.

Jack checked behind him. He put his hand on the emergency brake. Debbie saw, touched his hand and nodded.

He grazed the brakes. A horn blared behind him, and metal crunched, snapping Jack's head against his seat, but the Volvo scooted ahead. Their bumpers cleared, and Jack jerked the wheel to the right, pulling on the emergency at the same time.

The truck was on them before they started to roll.

*   *   *

Pain's the dark flip-side of excitement. It doesn't bore. It's always freshly minted. Blood in the wound glistens, and pain's world opens wide, all-encompassing. Jack squirmed on pain's hook, but there was no place to go, and he was all alone. Like Vanderdecken tied to the rudder off the weather-whipped coast of Africa, beating his way into the knives of wind, never arriving, never making port, and each wave a reminder of the death that had already claimed him. Like Sisyphus with his shoulder to the rock, unable to see around it, having no idea how long it would grind into his shoulder, how long his legs would quiver beneath him begging to collapse.

Pain, as long as it lasts, is unending.

*   *   *

"I never believe we will come back," said Debbie.

Jack stroked the wheel. It felt so good to feel anything, even the steering wheel.

"It makes me want to kiss everything around me," said Jack.

Automatically, he moved into the left lane. The sign said *Compton Only*, and he followed the curve around with all the other cars. Four lanes joined them on the left. The highway was congested, but moving well.

"Do you think he survived?" asked Debbie. "Do you think that it made any difference?"

"Maybe," Jack said. "At least for a moment."

They passed under a sign.

Debbie turned and grabbed his arm. "Did you see it, Jack! Did you see it?"

He was already checking his mirror and signalling. "Yeah."

The sign read, *Harbor Blvd. Disneyland exit/Left Lane, 1/2 mile.*

"It's an exit. Can we make it, Jack? Can you make the exit?"

Four lanes of solidly packed commuters moving at eighty miles per hour stood in between him and a way off the highway, the first exit they'd seen in who could guess how many years. At eighty, a half mile takes only twenty seconds.

Four bumper to bumper lanes. Twenty seconds, and the Harbor Blvd. exit into Anaheim and Disneyland.

"I think so," he said, as he made the first merge. "I'm good in traffic."

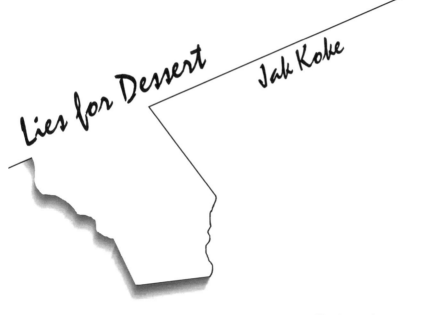

Mexican suddenly doubled over and fell, face first, out of the shade and onto the hot asphalt.

Trent tried to catch hold of Mexican's army fatigues to stop him from falling, but Trent's fingertips barely brushed the oil-stained fabric as it swept out of his grasp.

Mexican's emaciated body hit the asphalt and bounced, twisting unnaturally, his gaunt arms splayed wide to either side. He came to a rest faceup, his dark and sunken eyes staring into the scorching sun.

"Mexican?" Trent called.

No answer. No movement.

Trent pressed himself against the cool, corrugated metal of the abandoned warehouse, bracing to stand and walk out of the shade to check Mexican's pulse.

Had the man finally starved to death?

Trent gave up trying to stand when he saw the tiny men from inside the warehouse come in a single-file procession – chipmunk-sized humans parading out onto the hot asphalt. They marched single-file from between the sliding metal doors, around the big, green dumpster toward the spot where Mexican and Trent had camped out.

Trent leaned forward, squinting against the raw sun to get a closer look.

Tiny business suits and ties. Miniature cuff links and shiny shoes.

Trent wiped the sweat from his forehead and leaned back into the shade, the thin metal wall pressing hard into his spine. Magic. The little businessmen were more magic bullshit. Lies.

The creatures skirted the post of the cracked "Southern California Distributors" sign and the broken section of the dumpster's metal lid, goose-stepping past the heaps of yellowing paperbacks. They marched undaunted into the sun's scorching heat.

A beeline for Mexican's thin form.

Trent pulled his knees in against his chest. These tiny men were scavengers, come for Mexican's magic. Their presence proved that Mexican was indeed dead.

And Trent was alone again. Solo, for the first time since he'd met Mexican in the piss-smelling alley behind the 7-Eleven in downtown San Bernardino. Months ago, years maybe.

Time dilated on the street. How long ago had the driver thrown the two of them out of his big Cadillac, leaving them on a narrow road in the middle of the Mojave, saying that there was a truck stop just beyond the line of trees, but that this was as far as he could possibly take them?

How long ago – a week, a month? The driver's idea

of a joke had turned into miles of walking, hoping one of the few cars driving by would stop and take them back to civilization, until finally they'd come upon this warehouse. Shade. And water from the stream.

But the metal building was deserted, and locked up tight with a heavy chain. No trucks in sight. No sign of life except for the infestation of little men inside, occasionally peeking out through the crack in the sliding doors by the loading platform. Stopping to listen when Mexican told a story.

Now, as Trent examined the tiny executives, it seemed to him that their faces were familiar, as though long ago he'd known them. Or perhaps dreamt them. He hugged his knees tightly to hold off the shakes. Goddamn magic men. Can't eat them. Gotta find some food with substance. Something besides these paperbacks. Maybe then the shakes'll stay away.

The strong smell of deodorant soap and aftershave came with the procession, cutting like a clean blade through Mexican's thick urine odor and the ancient oil aroma of the asphalt lot. The clean smell interrupted the shakes, clotted in Trent's throat, reminding of him of the ad agency where he used to work. Years ago it seemed.

The first of the small creatures reached through the hole in Mexican's right work boot and poked the dead man rudely in the soft of his foot.

Mexican, splayed on his twisted back, gaunt face staring up at the hot and vacant sky, did not change expression. He did not twitch or flinch in his piss-stained army fatigues.

Mexican's magic had limited power to fend off death. That was clear now. Magic was storytelling and lies, for appearances, for escape. It was necessary for making novels and movies, but it couldn't replace food.

Mexican had been a good storyteller, and that's why the little men were coming, all clean and prim in the sweaty afternoon sun. They wanted his magic. They'd come to scavenge.

Now, fifteen or twenty of the creatures had reached Mexican and more were on their way. They formed a big circle around the body, each one thumping Mexican's flesh as though checking a melon at the supermarket. They wedged themselves under his bulk, focusing their strength where the bones jutted at sharp angles against his skin.

Then they lifted. The arm crews got their parts up right away, but leg group was having trouble with the baggy fatigues, and the others couldn't budge the man's torso. Too heavy. They waited for reinforcements.

A couple of the suits approached Trent tentatively, stopping and starting like wind-up robot toys. The one in the front had the face of Trent's ex-boss, Gary Swiney.

The doll-sized Gary punched him in the ankle bone with a sharp fist.

"Hey," Trent said. He kicked the Gary-doll sending him flying across the lot.

Gary-doll landed with a cartoon splat, bits of flattened suit and cuff links staining the pavement. The crowd let out a short controlled laugh in unison that sent a shiver of the heebie jeebies prickling along Trent's skin. Then the Gary-doll burst into a puff of paper — tax forms and interoffice memos. The cloud of forms floated away like smoke, disintegrating in the heat.

"Stay the fuck away from me." Trent reached back

to the pile of paperbacks that flowed from the dumpster and pulled one of the *Guiding Light* bibles to use as a weapon. Stripped of their covers, the books had yellowed and faded from overexposure to direct sun. Mexican had thought the mountain of paperbacks was the best thing about the place. He'd lived off those books for a long time. Mostly he'd eaten the Bibles. About half of them were Bibles.

When the hunger had first struck hard, Trent had tried the magic trick that Mexican used all the time. Tear out a page and use the illusion to make the Gospel look like a Big Mac and fries. Sometimes you could even smell the special sauce over the melting-asphalt odor. Trent had gotten halfway through Luke, and had sampled smatterings of Matthew and John when he realized that none of the magic he knew could make the books *taste* like anything other than the paper they were printed on. The magic had no power to change the paper into food. The sharp pains of hunger had continued to keep him awake.

Eventually he'd given up using the magic. The only paper that actually filled his stomach was the green kind imprinted with pictures of Lincoln or Jefferson. And Trent had run out of green a long time ago.

Trent shifted position, pulling his legs in until his knees touched his chest, trying to ignore the black hole in his gut. It all boiled down to food, didn't it? The magic meant nothing without nourishment. You can't enjoy a fantasy on an empty stomach. And you can't survive by eating books.

Trent remembered what it'd been like before the agency had laid him off. After spending all his savings to move out to Los Angeles, he hated his new job.

Monotony, boredom of the nine-to-five day to day. Nights alone. No friends. But there was one key difference between then and now.

Food.

He'd made money; he'd eaten every day.

Trent cleared sweat from his face with the back of his arm and scooted further into the ever-shrinking shade of the warehouse. More and more tiny men trailed around the dumpster to join in the effort. Must've been almost a hundred now and still they came, pristine suits with shiny, sweaty faces and blow-dried hair.

The tiny execs struggled to get Mexican's shoulders and mid-section off the ground. But the dead man's skin kept slipping as the suits tried to lift him, and the sagging folds of his fatigues tripped and tangled them.

Ever since Trent had met Mexican – the darker-skinned man offering Trent a big callused hand and a swig of Old English 800 – Trent had wondered whether those army fatigues were genuine. Whether Mexican, himself, was genuine. Was he really Latino or just a tan Caucasian or maybe some displaced Mediterranean homeboy? Since Mexican had never offered a name or an explanation, Trent just called him Mexican and figured that was the end of things.

Mexican rarely talked of his heritage and avoided the subject of Vietnam, but he *had* been full of stories. He talked nonstop whenever he wasn't eating.

And Trent listened. As he figured it, no one had ever listened to the man before. Mexican's stories carried them away from the harsh reality of their tight stomachs and the stench of their clothing.

Mostly Mexican spoke of his women, or he told a variation of the time his motorcycle was stolen by a gang of teenagers. In one version, Mexican tracked the gang to their hideout. Then he ambushed the thief and killed him with a crowbar. Or else, he called in the cops, or launched a one-man war using some dynamite that his old drug-trafficking friends had hidden years ago.

The story always changed, but that was okay. Trent needed something cheap to take his mind off his pain and humiliation. Drugs and alcohol weren't cheap. Mexican's tales helped carry him through.

One of Mexican's stories – Trent's favorite – was set in Hollywood, one of few places in the world where the magic was so strong that it made people rich. "The line between the real and the fantasy is blurry in those studios and sets," Mexican had said, pausing to light a cigarette. "I picked up my girlfriend (it seems odd to call her that now since we never saw each other afterwards) and we went to a special luncheon for some big-shot producer.

"We got there late, on account of some private back-alley driving I was giving my babe, if you know what I mean. And when we finally got to the club, everyone was in dresses or tuxes for fuck's sake, 'cept for me. I'd dressed up in a cleanish pair of 501s and a white muscle shirt. Had more bulk then.

"My girlfriend bitched at me about the clothes, but we got in anyway, and as soon you could say Jack-fucking-Frost, she'd disappeared into the crowd.

"So I was left to myself, which was cool. I just free-loaded for a while. And let me tell you, the food was kickass. There was sushi and Chinese stir-fry, and whole plates full of cheese and salads and snacks and all sorts of weird shit I didn't recognize. All the drinks were free, so I got a little drunk on margaritas and started listening in on conversations.

"It turned out that the party was really a dedication of some sort for a hotshot screenwriter who'd recently kicked off. Cancer or something. Or maybe suicide. No one seemed to know, or even care why he'd bitten it, but they *did* care that he'd been good with the magic.

"He'd been good enough to get rich, and even in Hollywood, money is more important than magic. As I went from conversation to conversation, absently looking for my girlfriend, I overheard things like '...wonder which parts are the most magical...' and 'Ooh, I hope I get part of his hands. He wrote the *best* love scenes.' And I realized that the stir-fry meat was really the writer's body. We were eating the bastard. Parceling out what was left of his old magic as it were. Fucking ruthless."

Mexican's dark eyes had widened into glowing brown wells. He brought the cigarette to his lips and sucked until the tip glowed deep red. "It made me sick at the time," he continued, wisps of smoke drifting from his mouth as he spoke. "I went to the pisser and almost threw up. Luckily, I stopped myself.

"See, Trent, I was kneeling there with my finger in my throat when I realized that I needed this dead man's magic. I went back to the party and stuffed myself. Picked up some good stories along the way."

Now *Mexican* was dead.

In front of Trent, the dark-skinned bag of bones rocked and shifted as the little men hoisted it to their shoulders. Two hundred tiny suits, cuff links and tie clips glittering like sparkling sand in the heat of the sun, twisting and moving like a carpet of sea anemones brushing Mexican's body towards the sliding metal doors.

They'd take the stinking corpse inside to their factory and process it for the magic, wouldn't they? The thought that crossed Trent's mind was not one of revulsion at his friend's dark corpse maggoted by tiny executroids rooting through it. His thought was one of need. Why was he letting them steal his food?

For the first time in days or weeks or years, Trent stretched his legs out and pushed to his feet, using the metal wall of the station as a crutch. He stood, shaking on weak, stiff legs that swam amongst the huge folds of the oversized slacks which used to fit him. He squinted into the brightness of the sun and moved toward Mexican's corpse.

He took one step. Then another, before his legs buckled under him.

Trent pitched forward into the searing heat of the sun. But he'd fallen towards Mexican's body. He squinted to see the outstretched arm of his friend, a bony hand extended toward him as though beckoning for Trent to save him.

Trent pushed to his knees, hands scalded by hot asphalt, and lunged for Mexican. He caught hold of the man's outstretched palm just as the execs pushed double-time.

The coldness of the dead man's hand nearly made Trent pull back. Mexican's hands had always been warm and big. Now the hand that Trent clasped in his own felt thin and brittle in its coldness. Trent held tight and pulled.

Mexican's body jerked as his arm snapped taut, tugging Trent forward face-first onto the melting blacktop.

Thick oil stench clogged his nostrils as he held his fist closed, resolved to hang on.

The crowd of tiny execs hung on and redoubled their efforts. They swarmed. Tiny clean hands grabbing loose skin; shiny leather shoes digging into the rough pavement.

Trent pulled, determined to win this once. He thought of all the battles he'd lost. His job. His possessions, his desire to live leaking out in a series of drunken nights, ending finally beaten and battered in a midnight alley with the muggers' shapes retreating.

Mexican had helped him then. Nursed him back to health. Saved his life. Now, as a dead man, he would save it again. Besides, Trent wasn't about to sit and watch the man's corpse become fodder for a colony of miniature ad men and red-tape jocks.

Trent twisted into a sitting position and shifted his weight to stop the momentum. Then he planted his heels, digging them in, one against the rust-frozen wheel of the green dumpster and the other on the pavement.

His feet held, and he mustered all his strength for a great heave, lifting Mexican and a score of little men attached to him. The body lurched into the air, flying towards him.

The sudden slack threw Trent back, his feet slipping out from underneath him. He landed hard on his butt, Mexican's sun-baked corpse flopping in his lap with a dead thud, squashing a score of tiny execs.

The little suits popped into puffs of tiny ledgers and memos. The papers drifted up around Mexican's body and vanished like smoke in the sunlight.

Trent sat in a daze for a few seconds until the miniature crowd rushed him like a Lego-sized Wall Street invasion, trying to reclaim its treasure. Trent dragged Mexican's body against the oncoming tide of suits and ties, setting the corpse in the shade, propped up against the volcano of paperbacks.

Silhouetted and dark against the backdrop of books, Mexican looked as he once had when he was alive. Not dead at all. Only sleeping. Then his head lolled back and sideways, slipping to an impossible position – a wide-eyed stare into the stark, pale death of the summer sky.

Trent kicked and stomped at the tiny invaders. Pressed suits flew and splattered the vacant lot, spotting the oil stains with their deodorant soap smell. Exploding into a blizzard of tax-form confetti. And still they came, flowing around his feet, climbing the books, determined to have their prize.

He scooped up armfuls of the dry, yellow paperbacks and hurled them at the riot. Making the suits dodge and bolt, but not retreat. He found the broken section of the dumpster's lid, leaning against the sign post, and heaved it up onto his shoulder.

Trent released the plate metal, heavy and flat, into the core of the crowd. It hit the pavement with a loud clang, laying waste to twenty or thirty of them.

Tiny paper cuts stung his ankles and feet as the little men died. Trent reached into the hurricane of ledgers, picked up the lid and struck again. And again, his skin burning feverishly, his head swimming with the heat, his muscles teetering on the edge of exhaustion, until only a handful of execs remained.

Those left recoiled finally, as a unit, each brushing itself off and disappearing around the dumpster and through the space between the warehouse doors. Trent was left alone with Mexican once more.

He collapsed to the ground, shivering and sweating, shaking from fatigue, breathing slowly to gather his strength.   Hours and days passed that were minutes to the rest of the world.   He might have sat there quivering until he died, but he feared the little suits would come back with reinforcements.

Finally, Trent stood.   He stripped Mexican of his army fatigues and his work boots.   Then he hoisted the naked corpse to his shoulder and set it as far up on the pile of books as he could.

He reached into the piss-stained fatigues and removed Mexican's matches.   He used no magic to change the appearance of the funeral pyre.   Mexican lay crooked and emaciated like a dark and wrinkled skeleton.

Trent yanked a match loose from the book and struck it against the emery strip.   "Goodbye," he whispered, choking the words through a dry, cracked throat and shriveled lips.   Then he set the burning match to the pile of books.

At first the fire burned slowly, but soon it was a hot blaze.   Trent watched romance novels and comic books, horror and new age, fantasy and suspense become food for the hungry flames.   The fire ate through Bibles and smut without discrimination.

The heat drove Trent to the far corner of the warehouse.   The flames crackled and hissed, blackening Mexican's skin, ripping into his flesh like red-hot knives. The fire lasted hours and days and weeks until finally, when the afternoon sun was setting – a glorious red glow in the western sky – only embers remained.

Mexican had been burned – crisped to black all over.

But when Trent peeled back the charcoaled skin, he discovered that some of the flesh was nicely cooked.

Trent ate all the good parts over the next few days. And when he'd finished, he felt stronger than he had in months. He used the dumpster's broken lid to dig a grave for what remained of the man's body. He made the grave deep in the dry dirt behind the lot, deep enough to deter anyone from disturbing it.

He cleaned himself up in the stream, and made his way around the corner of the building to sit by the side of the road and wait for a ride.

Most of a day and a few cars passed before someone stopped for him – a man in a baby blue pickup truck with a load of workers in the back.

Trent thanked the man and climbed in with the others, taking no more than the clothes on his back and the desire for food and companionship. Eating Mexican had given him some new magic, and he wanted to share it – his recently acquired talent for storytelling. For lying.